# WHERE'S YOUR HEAD?

# WHERE'S YOUR HEAD?

## Psychology For Teenagers

Dale Carlson
Hannah Carlson, M.Ed., C.R.C.
Illustrations By Carol Nicklaus

BICK PUBLISHING HOUSE    1998    MADISON, CT

First published by Atheneum in hardcover 1977
Published simultaneously in Canada by McClelland & Stewart, Ltd.
Manufactured in the United States of America

SECOND EDITION
Edited by Director Editorial Ann Maurer
Senior Editor Sharyn Skeeter
Book Design by Jennifer A. Payne
Cover Design by Greg Sammons

Library of Congress Cataloging-in-Publication Data

Carlson, Dale Bick.
    Where's your head : psychology for teenagers / Dale Carlson and Hannah Carlson : illustrations by Carol Nicklaus.
        p.        cm.
    Originally published: New York : Atheneum, 1977.
    Includes bibliographical references and index.
    ISBN 1-884158-19-6
    1. Adolescent psychology--Juvenile literature. 2. Adolescent psychiatry--Juvenile literature. 3. Psychiatry--History--Juvenile literature. 4. Adolescence [1. Psychology. 2. Psychiatry. 3. Adolescence.] I. Carlson, Hannah. II. Nicklaus, Carol. ill. III. Title.
BF724.C325  1998
155.5--dc21                                                                    97-31717
                                                                                      CIP
                                                                                       AC

**Completely Rewritten
And Updated For The Next Millennium**

IN
DEDICATION

To all the young people everywhere who have answered, sometimes painfully, always honestly, our questions about their lives and feelings for so many years. And to their parents, teachers, and the librarians who helped to organize groups for our dialogues.

To Toni Mendez, agent, mentor, and friend for her decades of love and faith. To Ann Maurer, editor, for her skill, tact, and constant support. To Jean Karl of Atheneum, who first believed in, guided, and published this book, great gratitude.

To our next generation: Sam, Chaney, Malcolm — and Shannon. May you have the strength and clarity to understand that behavior is catching.

With our love.

BOOKS BY DALE CARLSON

FICTION:
*The Mountain Of Truth*
*The Human Apes*
*Triple Boy*
*Baby Needs Shoes*
*Call Me Amanda*
*Charlie The Hero*
*The Plant People*

NONFICTION:
*Manners That Matter*
*Wildlife Care For Birds And Mammals*


with HANNAH CARLSON

NONFICTION:
*Living With Disabilities*
*Basic Manuals For Friends Of The Disabled*
    *6 Volume Series*
*Girls Are Equal Too—How To Survive: For Teenage Girls*

# CONTENTS

# Introduction:
# Just How Crazy Are You?

You probably aren't any crazier than anybody else. It's just that being a teenager is enough to drive most people out of their minds. It's like no other time in your life, most of you will be glad to know. Because while some of it is good and exciting, a lot of being in your teens is pure torture, outer conflict, inner chaos, and total confusion.

The major difficulty is that you are solving problems in three directions at the same time. Past, future, and present.

Consciously and unconsciously, you are still feeling the pulls and ties and conflicts from your early childhood, especially the past relationships with your parents (or lack of them) and the environment that made you whatever kind of nut you are today.

At the same time, you're trying to figure out the future — how to get independent of your parents and your past; how to operate on your own. You take a look at the adult world and the mess it's in and wonder if you even want a future. Then you take another look, and decide you can do something about yourself and the world, and maybe you do want a future. That is, if you can figure out what kind.

And then there's the third direction. Right now. What is going on with you and where are you right now? This direction is particularly difficult since no teenager ever feels the same way ten minutes in a row. (Don't take this personally. You're growing and changing so fast and in so many directions, it makes the head spin.)

And to add to this overburden of inner confusion, you still have to survive the outer world: the struggle not to lose your place among your friends and in school; the physical, psychological, sexual harassment; the violence; the drugs, dealers, the drug scene in general; street crime. Some days it's an Olympic triumph just to make it home alive and get your homework done before: a) your parents start a fight with you; b) get drunk and divorce each other; c) kick you out of the house; d) escalate all these little internal, inhouse wars into an international conflict.

If you're lucky, you have a close friend or sympathetic parents or a teacher or somebody to talk to about the really hard things: peer pressure, sex, drugs; what you're going to do for a future (if you're going to have a future); about death and god and money; will-anybody-ever-love-me-or-will-I-be-lonely-for-the-rest-of-my-life. All of these are the things people really think about while they're saying something else.

If you're not so lucky, you may be bottling up all the anxiety inside you. You look at the most popular boys and girls in school and envy them because they seem to be handling things so easily while you're kickboxing demons. But they're going through the same stuff you are. They may just be coping better. A lot of the way you cope now has to do with how you learned to cope when you were very young.

Feeling lonely, separate, apart, different from other people (aside from real poverty, real physical pain) is probably the worst. You know the feeling. As if you were living in a private jail, at the bottom of a pit, somewhere you couldn't get out of and no one could get inside of to reach you, comfort you, keep you company. The loneliness can attack you even when you're with your friends, even when you're wearing the same things, talking the same language. Something inside you makes you feel as if you were struggling with something private and special. You are. You're trying to find out what your self is all about, and it's a lonely, private, and special struggle.

There's fear, anxiety, even panic. You can't stay home with your parents forever, but you're scared of the world out there. That you won't make it. That you can't. That you haven't got what it takes to cope with your future or even to call up somebody you're crazy about and ask for a date.

There are your dreams. The glory of your plans and how to make them happen. And the despair of not even being good enough to pass a math test or make a team or some days get it together to get out of bed.

And what do you do with your anger? At your friends for hurting your feelings; at enemies you'd like to kill; at parents who curb your independence or who don't seem to understand how much you still need them, who are either too much there or never there; at teachers for blocking you; at the whole world for having it in for you personally.

Joy; sometimes there's joy. Those hours of pure heaven when everything is right. And love, for someone in particular or just because of a perfect sunset. What do you do with an emotion you're so full of you're ready to explode? You can't go around hugging everyone in sight. How do you share things like that?

There are guilts about the things you've felt or done wrong, cheating, lying, hurting someone else, the shame and the fear of being found out. There's the confusion of loving and hating someone at the same time. There's the need to be free, yet the need to be safe. The grief (it's real!) over losing your childhood — and the excitement of becoming an adult. The private worries over how well or how little you've developed physically compared to everybody else — and the public worries over the state of the world and your natural need to help others.

Madness? The jumble of thoughts, feelings, and what may even seem like weird patterns of behavior sometimes may make you think you are losing your grip. But everybody goes a little mad during times of crisis — and adolescence, from about eleven to about twenty, can be the biggest crisis, because it's the time of the biggest change of your life.

How do you know if you're normally crazy or abnormally crazy? By the intensity of your reactions, by how long they persist, by whether they interfere seriously with your relationships, with your ability to function in school, at home, socially.

We all share the same feelings: fear, anger, pleasure, shame, guilt, being tired, hungry, lonely, joyful. Whether we express those feelings in English or Chinese, or express them in a scream or a whisper, in music or sports, or stuff them and not express them at all, people's feelings are everywhere and at all ages the same. Human beings, black, white, fast, slow, quarterbacks and violin players, all belong to the same species, and we are as alike as a colony of ants. (Go up in a ferris wheel or an airplane and look down.) Certainly, we are all more alike than unalike. Knowing we share emotions helps us to understand each other, despite the differences in patterns of behavior. **And learning about mental processes and those patterns of behavior is the whole purpose of psychology — so that you can free yourself from your mental pain!**

One truth here is that if you understand yourself, you can understand everybody else since we're all pretty much the same in the brain, give or take a few points of IQ, a few talents, a dash of hormones. It's exciting, when you come to think about it. To unlock the key to everyone's brain by understanding your own.

A second truth here, and what's in it for you, is that understanding yourself and everybody else is the key factor to survival. How are you going to survive in a world impossible to survive in? Understand it. Understand it by understanding yourself. Don't waste time blaming your parents and teachers for not teaching you about the nature of the self. They may not know. They may only have technical knowledge, scientific, social, or outer knowledge, not inner. You'll have to teach yourself. The way to do this is simply by observing yourself in your daily life, your daily relationships, by keeping certain questions in your mind about yourself, by being aware of your thoughts and feelings and behaviors. Just watch yourself in operation with others, with work, and listen to yourself.

- Does it seem you have a lot of different voices in your head talking to each other and all your various selves argue with each other all the time?

- Do you have the sneaking suspicion you're empty, there's nobody at home, when they tell you to find yourself, be yourself, and you look down your shirt and you can't find anybody, only a hole? That's why you spend a lot of time trying to fill that hole with food, talk, business, people, drugs, alcohol, work, sports, TV, music, whatever.

Believe your own observations! You're absolutely right! There are lots of selves in your brain (even science has confirmed there are lots of areas in the brain where information is taken in and processed, not one central information center). Your brain is full of tape-recorded announcements it has taken in during its whole life, from babyhood to yesterday. It is full of the history of our species, all the messages of millions of years of biological history. There are also gender messages, and racial messages, and cultural messages in your brain. And there are conscious, voluntary parts of your brain, the parts that can choose to learn a second language or the pieces of a car's engine — and unconscious, involuntary parts that control your breathing, responses to pain, and so forth.

So. The point is not, be your self (there are so many!). The point is to find out what your self (or selves) is all about, and not let it (or them) drag you down blind alleys like wild horses. You don't want to be driven by all those thoughts and feelings based on old messages from everybody else in your brain, or even your own old experiences. You want your actions based on intelligence. (Intellect is just thought, memorized stuff, always old; intelligence is the ability to see it, get it, whatever it is, right now.)

The brain does two things: it thinks and it understands. The brain's job is to protect the body, to keep it safe. You need memory and thought or you wouldn't be able to talk or find your way home or make a cheese sandwich. But you need intelligence, understanding, to live right.

Thought (old stuff) and intelligence (right-now observation) are two separate things. The dumb person is not the one who doesn't understand books, but the one who doesn't understand herself or himself. Understanding comes only through self-knowledge, which is awareness of one's total psychological process. Education, in the true sense, is this understanding of the ways of oneself and everyone else, not just information in books.

The first edition of this book was about general psychology. Now, because what you will learn in schools are mostly only skills to make a living, we need to talk about skills in living. If you're going to live at all in this increasingly exciting but difficult world.

At home, the main job seems to be teaching you mostly how to fit into society, but what we need to talk about is how to change this society that exploits everything and everyone when it should be nurturing everything and everyone.

The world is more dangerous now and more complex. So the purpose of this new edition twenty years later is more serious. It is not just about psychology, but psychological survival.

*Section One*

---

# THE PERSONAL YOU

Everybody's mind is a battleground. The trouble is that most of the time we can't locate the enemy. More of the time, we can't even locate the battleground. That's because most conflicts take place in the unconscious, not the conscious (aware) part of our mind. For instance:

*Janie is an easy ten pounds overweight. Her jeans are so tight they're uncomfortable to sit down in, and her mother makes her miserable by calling her a slob and telling her*

*that no boy will ever date a fat girl. In school, in the hall-
ways, boys make fun of her body as if she weren't there, as if
all she was was her body and not also the sweetest flute player
and best basketball guard in town. Janie hates the way she
looks, hates being reminded she is overweight, hates it so
much that in fact most of the time she is miserable. So miserable that she comforts herself with the one thing that comforts her — and at the same time destroys her — food! Sometimes she tries to diet and loses a few pounds. But if something goes wrong, she starts eating again, grows even more
depressed. She has begun to mutilate herself secretly with
small razor cuts because the physical pain helps minimize
the psychological pain, and thinks about ways of suicide.*

To Janie's thin friend Marcelle, it doesn't seem like much
of a problem. Just stop eating for a while and lose twenty
pounds. But Marcelle doesn't understand the personal identity battleground of Janie's unconscious. Neither she nor
Janie knows why Janie needs to eat even when the conscious
part of her wants to be thin.

But then neither of them understands Marcelle's problem, either.

*Up until about the eighth grade, Marcelle had always got-
ten very good marks in school, especially in math and science. She had often talked about being a doctor. In the past
year or so, Marcelle's marks have dropped from A's and B's
to C's. Not because Marcelle isn't trying. She is working
hard. But very often, the day before a test, Marcelle gets*

*sick. Or she comes to the test twenty minutes late, unavoidably delayed. Or she actually forgets assignments or loses a term paper. None of these things are her fault, consciously.*

Joe, Marcelle's boyfriend, can't figure it out. If Marcelle wants to be a doctor the way she says she does, she's going to have to pull her marks together for college. So why does Marcelle pull all this dumb stuff?

Getting good marks is no problem for Joe. But there is a little something about himself he doesn't get.

*Why does he feel so worthless when he looks at himself in the mirror? He gets good marks. He's captain of the swimming team. He writes for the school newspaper. He heads school service committees and charity drives, organizes school dances, has good friends, knows he's attractive. So why does he feel inadequate? Why does he have to keep on doing more and more things to keep that worthless feeling away? And why is there that constant anger in him? Who is he angry at all the time?*

The discovery of the importance of the unconscious in driving our behavior was Sigmund Freud's greatest contribution to the understanding of human behavior in the Western world. (In the East, they've known about this for thousands of years — they call it karma.) But here, until Freud, the founder in the Western world of modern depth psychology, began practicing medicine in the 1890's, and then Carl Jung, Otto Rank, Alfred Adler, and later on in our time, Erik Erikson, Peter Blos, Dorothy Briggs, Karen Horney, Arnold Gesell, it was not known that most mental activity is unconscious. That most of our conflicts and a lot of our behavior is directed by the unconscious, unaware part of our minds. Only a small part of our mental activity is conscious, like the tip of an iceberg. The rest — such as early childhood experiences and emotions, inherited species and racial memories, subliminal cultural messages — we're either born with or pushed below the surface. It remains repressed or unknown, and is not recalled by the conscious mind.

But just because we have no access to our ancient biological brain memory, or because we have fought down certain feelings or can't remember how it felt to be six months old doesn't mean those memories, emotions, and experiences aren't there — and not only there, but hollering for expression. Nothing that ever happens or has happened to you (eons of it!) ever disappears. It simply is already underground or goes there later on to harass you. Some of it is good. For instance, if you got a lot of warm cuddling and nice, satisfying sucking experiences when you went through your first year of life, you will probably, unless something else went wrong later, end up a warm, trusting, generous person. If your first year or two were difficult, and you got rejected or received less affection than you needed, you could end up desperate for love, depressed, possibly a drug addict, an alcoholic. If you were truly abandoned, you might become a sociopath with no sympathy for other people at all. It's difficult enough choosing not to exploit or kill, because our biological inheritance makes us predators. But if, on top of that, you've had an abused childhood, and even if you've stuffed the memories, you'll live the results, perhaps by abusing others or seeking abusive situations yourself. Both nature and nurture, genetic inheritance and environment, shape your brain and your personality in ways we don't fully understand.

Clearly, the behavior of Janie, Marcelle, and Joe cannot be understood without first understanding that we only seem to be in touch with about 15% of our brains, that 85% of our brains remain inaccessible to most of us. Consciously, all three want to be comfortable with themselves, to be free of anxiety (that feeling ranging from uneasiness to fear), to do freely what their aware minds want to do. But in each case, something is hanging them up, something they can't get at or understand. Forces in their unconscious minds are pulling them in directions they don't want to go.

Does Janie eat so much because unconsciously she needs to punish herself (by staying fat) for some past, unremembered guilt? And why choose eating too much as the punishment? Is her food addiction the kind of comfort she craves to make up for a less-than-loving babyhood? Is she afraid of the world, boys, sex, pregnancy, and wants to keep people away from her by staying fat?

And Marcelle. Is her sudden inability to work mostly influenced by sexism, the unconscious, programmed-in need to fail in order to be feminine that damages so many girls? And if so, is it because of her parents' influence, the media, the need for approval measured by dating success not personal achievement, that so poisons girls' minds in our culture?

No matter how much Joe does, he still feels inadequate. Unknown needs force him to do more and more, but nothing makes him feel satisfied with himself. Who is he trying to please? Who is holding the whip at his back? We can be certain that when we find the person in Joe's unconscious who's holding that whip, we'll also know who he's angry at.

Before you can plunge into what can go wrong with personality formation, it helps to understand really well what goes into the structure of personality. It makes it easier to divide the personality into three parts:

1. animal, biological inheritance
2. personal experience
3. cultural inheritance

Counseling and therapy can help with some of the difficult treasure hunt. Yet most of what's down there we can find out by watching ourselves right now, today, in the mirror of our relationships with others! (Some days you want to kill? There's the hunter/predator/killer animal in you right there! Some days you want to kidnap your boyfriend or girlfriend so no one else can ever have them? There's the territorial ancient mating urge!) But there is other training/conditioning in your psyche (the word is from the Greek, meaning "mind" or "soul"). You can listen for yourself to the conflicts and the opposing forces in your head. Some of it is buried deep, but you can get enough to understand the rest down below.

## Animal, Biological Inheritance

This contains the raw, basic, primitive, animal stuff you were born with, the biological urges of sex and aggression, the need to eat, breathe, and to eliminate, the need to be loved, to grow. After all, the main job of the brain is to protect and nurture the organism, to keep you alive. These functions of the brain are mostly unconscious, like breathing, or the needs for food, warmth, shelter, safety, sex, urges that demand satisfaction if you are to stay alive and reproduce. These urges are full of energy. They are your life force. It's only when we demand not just enough, but more than our share that they become destructive.

During a lot of the first year of your life, you are mainly these basic urges: to eat, to eliminate, to be held close and safely. Usually, a lot of kicking and screaming will get you what you want. But as you get a little older and your drives get more complicated, kicking and screaming don't help much. You can't always release your sexual energy in a direct way. You can't hit everybody in sight when you're mad. And there are other basic urges.

Jung was the psychologist in the West who described what Moses and Jesus, Buddha and Lao-Tse, Mohammed and the Vedas and goddesses everywhere have understood since the dawn of humanity: that we have an instinct as basic as the need to eat to fulfill our natures (fill that hole!) by reaching out beyond our loneliness and uniting with god, the universe. Metaphysicists and physicists, religious people and scientists, are part of the same quest for the same truth. A basic instinct seems to be an instinct for immortality in us all, said Rank and many others.

How are you to gratify all that? How can you give your greedy needs what they want, desperately, constantly? All that psychic energy can be very pushy! To deal with it, the human brain cleverly develops other parts of itself. So that sexual energy can be turned into work. So aggression can be let out by hitting a ball with a bat instead of hitting someone's head with a bat. So that we can fulfill our own natures by growing, by reaching out to other people, or in silence, connecting with nature, god, the universe.

## Personal Experience

In babyhood, basic needs are met or not met, trust in the world develops or it doesn't. But as the nervous and muscular systems develop, the brain develops more complex capacities to help you get what you want.

The ego, or self, begins to develop. Really, the self is a collection of selves that seems to have elected a gang leader. It is not true that there is a leader or a homunculus (a little person) in there, but it feels that way. This ego is mostly conscious; it is the part of your personality that is most aware of what is going on around you, the reality principle. Like a computer, it takes account of the facts and gives you the answers. Such as when to cross a street to the Mall, whether you can afford a motorcycle, and if you can get away with smacking your little sister or skipping school to play computer games. The ego chooses what's important for you to understand in the world, what your senses should take in, what's dangerous and what's not dangerous, what you logically should do and what you shouldn't do about dating, drugs, school, your parents, dropping out, plugging in, living your life.

This self is the part of you that you call by name, the one on the wristband they gave you at the hospital when you were born or the one you picked up later on the street or in school. This self does more than size up what's going on outside you. It also sizes up what's going on inside you. It's your self that stands between the needy greedies of your biology and the actualities of the world.

Biological self:    *I want to murder Marcelle, she's so thin.*

Personal self:    *They'll throw you in the slammer for that. Stick your tongue out at her instead.*

The personal self develops all kinds of defense mechanisms against the dangerous biological impulses. We'll talk about those later on. During a normal childhood, the personal self develops strength and learns to satisfy your instinctive needs in ways that do not get a person into trouble. (A one-year-old will learn just how much hollering it can get away with in order to get food without at the same time driving its mother to refuse ice cream. Experience will also find new ways to get that food and satisfy needs without hollering — like cooing and being adorable instead.)

As the personal self develops, the need to satisfy your needs, and your understanding the realities of what the world will let you have, work together in guiding behavior. The relative strength of each will determine most of your personality.

Of course, the pressure on your conscious self may make you misunderstand the realities of the outer world and therefore not let your self work properly. Because not only do you have to cope with the demands of your basic instincts to survive, you have to cope with the third of the three agendas — the social, ethnic, gender, family, in short, the cultural stuff they put in your brain.

## Cultural Inheritance

This force develops later than the other two, around the age of five or six. The cultural messages you receive become roughly the voices of your conscience and the knowledge of what your background says is right and wrong. But it's more than that. Along with your basic drives and your self's needs, the conscience helps to inspire you to behave rightly because it's the right thing to do, not just because you'll get a smack if you don't. Some people call this a kind of god-connection, or the "still, small voice," or the universal intelligence that speaks through us all.

Until you were five or six, in general you had to go along with what your parents told you to do or not to do. After all, you weren't a lot of feet tall, and you didn't have a nickel to your name.

*"No, George. We paint on the paper, not on the wall. (That didn't make much sense to you, but the spanking did.)*

*"No, Bertha, we do not put little berries in the keyhole. See? Now the key won't fit." (Who cared about the berries? But you did learn about no more television for a week.)*

*"No, Darien. Mommy doesn't like it when you hang your brother out the window by his overall straps." (You may not like your brother, but your mother likes him enough to give you time out against the wall for a year.)*

*"Jimmy, what a beautiful picture!" (Beautiful? Same smear you did yesterday with the finger paints. But the praise feels good, and you make a mental note to do a few more smears.)*

*"Lisa, how nice of you to give your baby brother your truck." (Nice? You only did it because you just hit him and you didn't want him to cry and get you into trouble. But the approval felt good. Make a note to be nicer to the little creep.)*

And the yes, no, yes, no goes on until you hit one of the more major crises of your childhood around the age of four for boys, a touch later for girls. He decides he'd like to have his mother all for himself without his father for competition, and she'd like to keep her father. This is perfectly natural. When you are struck with these very early sexual feelings, what more natural than to turn to whomever is handy, close, nice to you. But this happy instinct is the no-no of all time. Society has absolutely forbidden that particular one, and at about the point this dawns on you, you begin to develop inside voices that tell you what's right and wrong in your culture and what kind of person you ought to be. What you do is internalize parent and society voices so that they are now a part of your own psyche. These voices are your conscience, which makes you feel good when you're "good" and guilty and ashamed when you're "bad." Much of your conscience is unconscious, partly because the voices were drummed into you very early and your nervous system recorded them without necessarily understanding or sorting them out. (Why the last is so important, is that being a "good" girl or "good" boy may not always be the same as right living. Finding partners besides your family is genetically sound. Killing because your culture says to make riots or war may not be, no matter what your society says. Maturity is the understanding of the difference between being a "good" girl/boy, and goodness. Now, in your teens, is an excellent time to begin sorting out your cultural agenda and deciding for yourself what voices to listen to and what to shut up.)

As you can guess, the three parts of your brain are often in conflict.

BASIC DRIVE: *"I want!"*

SELF-EGO (reality computer): *"Better not, you'll get hurt."*

CULTURAL CONSCIENCE: *"You can't do it because it's wrong."*

When the basic drive wants something, often the conscience comes down hard on it. This makes the drive try to find other ways to satisfy itself, with the help of the ego. From these conflicts come the source of behavior.

BASIC DRIVE: *"I'm angry."*

CULTURAL CONSCIENCE: *"Murder is strictly out!"*

SELF-EGO: (healthy) *"Talk about it. Bang a trash can."*

SELF-EGO: (either weak or unhealthy) *"Kick the dog. Take it out on your friend. Punish yourself by getting depressed or a headache or hurting yourself with people, places, addictions."*

The cultural conscience is not a force of reality. It is the so-called moral force, voices you heard long ago judging your behavior now. The judgments may be too easy (allowing us to behave irresponsibly), too hard on us and push us (like Joe) to prove ourselves over and over, almost beyond endurance, just to earn our right to breathe air. *These are the voices most in need of examination by the ability we all have to observe ourselves.*

### Connection to the Universe

The fourth drive is powerful, a force so basic it is often ignored. It is our need to connect, to matter in and to the universe, whether you call it god, the stars, the goddess, the ALL. The fact that our brains are too limited to understand that everything is connected, therefore everything matters, drives us crazy. Because we don't see the importance of each link, each atom to every other atom, we scramble for importance, often at the environment's expense, sometimes at each other's expense, always at our own expense. We also don't see that the brain does two things: it thinks, accumulating knowledge; but also, it has the very intelligence that is connected to the intelligence of the universe.

So. As you see, all the various selves, voices, conflicts argue with each other inside your head all the time you are awake, and even when you sleep, in your dreams. No wonder you're psychologically exhausted. No wonder you want the music loud!

### Defense Mechanisms

When the conflicts between the four forces we've mentioned (there may be more, this is just a working model), produce too much anxiety or chaos, the ego goes to work. It works to defend us against too much anxiety by using unconscious defense mechanisms that began to develop back in early childhood. The use of defense mechanisms is perfectly usual, because none of us has been taught early on, along with reading, writing, and the color of an apple, the nature of the human being and its brain. We all use these defense mechanisms against pain and confusion instead, to reduce anxiety, to block out disturbing memories. Some lessen temptation, some transform the cravings of our biological needs into a form that is easier for the conscience to approve of. Defense mechanisms make your personality more stable, but they can also create problems and disturbed behavior when they become too rigid or fixed. Defense mechanisms deeply influence thought, behavior, and personality development.

D*enial.* This is just plain ordinary rejection. We simply do not acknowledge the existence of something painful, or we lie to ourselves about it. Janie, for instance, would really like to have a boyfriend as Marcelle does. But it's too painful for Janie to admit she's lonely, and afraid of intimacy besides. Instead, she says she's just not interested in boys yet and denies the hurtful emotions.

*Repression.* This mechanism is not just denial. It is a more complicated process that forces unwanted or unacceptable experiences, emotions, wishes down into the unconscious and keeps them there. Repressed emotions powerfully influence our behavior, but because they are unconscious we aren't aware of them. Joe doesn't know that he tries so hard in school to please a severe and critical father. On the surface he doesn't like his father much. But two repressed emotions drive Joe on. A deep love for his father from early childhood that results in a need for his father's approval. And a forbidden anger at the whip he feels cracking over his head. Both the love and the anger are repressed, too painful for Joe to accept consciously.

*Projection.* We all do this often. You feel an emotion you don't want to feel, so you blame it on someone else. It's not you who's angry, it's your mother who's angry at you. It's not you who's wrong, the whole world is conspiring against you. People who project too much feel that everyone is always attacking them for no reason, that nothing is ever their own fault.

*Displacement.* It's that old kick-the-other-kid business when you're really annoyed at your parents. Displacement is the transference of emotion from one object, situation, or person to another. If you resented your parents' authority a great deal during your childhood, it is likely you will resent the authority of teachers now, and displace that same resentment to all future authority figures.

*Conversion.* Transferring a psychic ache to a bellyache. If the history test is going to be a pain in the head, turn it into a pain in the stomach instead. Afraid you can't jump the hurdles at the track meet? A temporary paralysis of the legs will take care of this. Strong emotional conflicts can be converted to physical symptoms. (This is called psychosomatic behavior, somatizing.)

*Reaction formation.* This is a cute one and not too hard to detect in your friends. It means covering up something you don't like in yourself by forming the exact opposite trait. The too-too adorable, sweet, polite lady or the too-too charming gentleman may very well be sitting on enough hostility, hate, and fury to blow up the Western world. That muscley macho type who bullies everyone may be soft as a marshmallow inside. The person who is scrubbed at all times and never says a four-letter word may be afraid to face an internal, psychic pig.

*Regression.* A retreat to earlier levels of behavior. Have you ever seen adults on New Year's Eve? At Disney World? Ever seen adults use tears, temper tantrums, whining to get what they want? Cigarette smoking, alcohol, drugs, overeating, all satisfy regressive needs that go back to the first year of life, replacements for sucking on a bottle. Severely ill mental patients may totally regress to infantile behavior, but nobody is free of it entirely. Most of us use this mechanism from time to time when the going gets tough and it's just easier to be childish for a while.

*Fixation.* The refusal to grow beyond a certain phase of development. Anything from never getting toilet-trained to refusing to leave home and learn to live an independent life. You can get fixated at any stage in your life, sometimes temporarily, sometimes permanently.

My two favorite defense mechanisms are the most pleasant and self-satisfying of the lot, sublimation and rationalization. They make for most of my own personal obsessions!

*Sublimation.* The use of all the basic drives, whether to get angry or get sex, in happier ways. People with strong sexual drives may use a lot of that energy to write books or create a new business.

*Rationalization.* The joy of finding a perfectly logical reason that makes you look good when you were really nasty to someone, or a reason for doing something you probably shouldn't do but want to do anyway without letting your-self in on the secret. You absolutely need that new shirt or that pair of skates or a new car. And since it's on sale, you can explain to your mother that you saved her somewhere between $1.95 and $850, thereby making you both very happy without anybody having to admit you're a vain, greedy child. Rationalization is often one of the self's ways of defending itself against a too-strong emotion, like shame or guilt. There are people who are able to intellectualize feel-ings to the vanishing point.

*Humor*, a marvelous defense mechanism, is a good outlet for anxiety, a relief from grim reality. But watch out for people who make jokes in your face every time you express an emo-tion, or always joke when they express their own.

Especially watch out for people who make jokes at other people's expense. Humor can be a form of hate, from mild put-down to outright genocide.

*Daydreaming* is another good one. You can get a lot of what you want from a good imagination without having to worry about conflicts.

Add to the various selves, the basic drives, the personal experiences, the cultural voices, the following forces: religions (these respond to our needs for immortality and our fears of death); nationalism (an outgrowth of the family, the community, more basically, even, the herd, the pack, an instinct in the human species like wolves and zebras for pro-tection by belonging). Add also your talents and capacities, whether for growing tomatoes, the high jump, playing the keyboard, or nuclear physics.

So this is the nature of the self, of you, of all of us — all the inherited and acquired voices and experiences of millions of years as well as your own particular life. As you can see, the self (we'll call all those selves just "self" now, for convenience) protects itself in complicated ways. It is full of chaos and conflicts, truths and half-truths and lies, suffering, anxiety, pleasure; all the bits and pieces of you fighting all the other bits and pieces of you. It is not a single identity, even though it feels like one. There is not a single you, even though it feels as if there is a single you. (Have you ever had the feeling you have to pull yourself together in your head? Collect your self? That's because the nature of the self is bits and pieces, not a single entity. And besides, there are all those gaps between thoughts and voices. There isn't even continuity.) There are times YOU aren't even there. Make love, watch a beautiful sunset, and you get some relief from your selves — until you pull yourself together again.

But those gaps, lovely as they are, can be scary. In the absence of self, if you let it happen, you really are connected with love and the universe and all out there (some people call these states of being prayer and meditation and peace and freedom, and everyone says they want these states, but not many really do because it scares them). This is why the self protects itself in complicated ways.

Getting beyond this self, even from time to time, requires a lot of observation of its own ways. Just not letting the self become too neurotic (developing self-defeating patterns of behavior) or psychotic (losing contact with reality) is hard enough.

Most people, you've noticed by now, act not from love or even affection for their friends, children, lovers, husbands, wives, but from fear. Fear of losing face, fear of losing possession, fear of losing control, fear of losing some precious image of themselves, fear of being alone, fear of death. It's thinking, our thoughts, that produce these fears as well as all the selves.

Can we learn to act from love instead of fear? Can we learn to behave for the general good, instead of just self-protection?

But let's start from the beginning of you and your self. Because if you don't understand your brain, it will kill you and others. Its contents can do that by pushing and pulling you in terrible and terrifying directions. And you won't know it until it's too late.

Clarity, understanding, is the antidote. It will help you stop wasting yourself.

Begin with the baby in you.

*Section Two*

---

# EARLY
# CHILDHOOD

# The Baby In You

The baby in you, the child in you, is still there, and will be there the rest of your life. NOTHING THAT HAS EVER HAPPENED TO YOU OR THE WAY YOU FELT ABOUT IT EVER DISAPPEARS! It is all there, in your unconscious, stored away either to plague you or help you as long as you live. You can change the way you behave about it all, but few human beings have ever totally transformed the self and all its stuff.

During your babyhood you didn't have words and other mental abilities to create conscious memories. During your early childhood, you couldn't cope with certain experiences and strong feelings. Your nervous system was too immature. So in those years, until about the age of six, you repressed like crazy. And since those six years are the most important of all in terms of early personality development, they are the years that drive you crazy later on.

(I use the word "crazy" a lot. I shouldn't. Mental health is a matter of degree, and there are no sharp divisions anymore between what people used to call sane and insane. When I use the word crazy, I just mean those moments or days or problems that make you feel as if you're hanging on by your fingernails.)

In the first year of our lives, the great need, the greatest joy, is to suck on something. Not only for nourishment — important enough — but for the sheer pleasure a baby gets from a mouth. A baby will put anything and everything into its mouth. If there's no breast or bottle immediately available, pacifiers, blanket corners, blocks, its own fingers and toes — anything will do. But the joy of nursing is the best, because from that the baby gets two things it needs: food and love. To be held, cuddled, kept warm and close is the beginning of a baby's sense of being an okay person in an okay world. The sucking of food relieves hunger and tension, but it's the loving and holding and trusting its needs will be met that make a baby bloom. Institutionalized babies who were properly fed have been known to shrivel and die simply from lack of loving and touching; and in experiments with animals, when babies have been removed from their mothers or orphaned, the same thing has happened. Babies rejected by their mothers for any number of possible reasons often go into infantile depression from which some of them never entirely recover. Orphaned or badly fostered children who are sent from place to place, children abandoned in wars, these often suffer language and thinking disabilities from lack of stimulation. Worse, they suffer attachment disorders from lack of bonding, some becoming sociopathic (without conscience or empathy for the pain of others).

Inadequate loving can occur in many ways and is not always the mother's fault:

*Susan was her mother's sixth child. Her birth was accidental, and her mother was just plain tired. With five other children, the housework, and marital problems to cope with, there just wasn't time or energy enough to do more than feed Susan quickly and put her back, crying, into her crib. And the more Susan cried, the more guilty, annoyed, and angry her mother became. During Susan's childhood, she was a good, obedient, helpful child. (Rejected children, if they don't withdraw entirely from human relationships, often try harder for the approval of and become more dependent on the rejecting parent.) When Susan entered her early teens, a time when we all unconsciously relive the conflicts of our first years, her behavior changed. She was never home. She spent all her time with a close girl friend older than she (a substi-*

*tute mother image for the mother who had rejected her) and experimented with alcohol (a new bottle substituted for not being allowed to suck long enough on an earlier bottle). No one understood her sudden bad behavior, of course. She had always been such a good girl! Chemical imbalances like an inability to metabolize alcohol (alcoholism) ran in the family, so that was her addiction of choice, but nobody understood that, either.*

Nobody's fault, really. The mother needed help as much as the daughter.

*Dana's mother was told to nurse by the doctor, as mother's milk helps to provide a baby with the proper immunizing agents against disease. But Dana's mother didn't really want to nurse. It hurt her nipples. It tied her more than she wanted to be tied to the baby. She did it anyway for five months under doctor's orders, and then, only on schedule, not when Dana needed to be fed and cuddled. Dana as a baby knew nothing of her mother's pain and restless nature. She simply reacted to what she experienced as rejection. Like Susan, she was a good, obedient child. But then in her mid-teens, she began to have depressions (reliving the earlier depression) which she found could be helped by only one thing: what she called love. The love she didn't feel when she was a child she now found in the love of a boy. Not a normal, healthy love based on common interests and mutual respect and equality. Dana picked boys who were of lesser intellect and background, because like all rejected children, she had a low sense of self-worth. Besides, she had to get out from under her dependency on her mother. And dating objectionable boys was one way of letting out her anger, by rejecting her mother's standards. Her basic need was to find a needy boy so that he would give her the love she had never felt from her mother. Like Susan, Dana had other problems that came from being fixated on (not outgrowing) the unmet needs of her babyhood. There was always something in her mouth. She was always either drinking something or eating something or smoking or chewing her nails or talking too much. Her mouth never stopped. As Dana grows older, some kind of addiction is probable, to food, to chemicals, to people. One indication of her intense dependencies is her habit of attaching herself to people like a tick.*

Dana's mother claims that she always loved Dana very much, that Dana was simply a difficult teenager. Most mothers claim they love their children, even if many parents are too concerned with their own problems to love, even if they haven't, as most of us don't, the slightest idea what love is. But if the child doesn't feel that love, it doesn't matter that the love was there. Sometimes, no matter how much affection a mother gives, it seems not to be enough, some babies seem to be almost unsatisfiable. Genetically, all babies inherit different intellectual, emotional, and physical endowments. Mothers and babies sometimes just don't match. The point is, things can go wrong in you that aren't necessarily your parents' fault. Psychology is an exploration of causes, not a science for let's-hang-our-parents techniques. As Peter Blos says, "Trauma [shocks to the system] is a universal phenomenon of childhood." Meaning, even if you have terrific parents, you've got problems. But although one quality of mentally healthy people is that they outgrow each stage of development instead of getting unconsciously stuck there, nobody ever seems to outgrow everything.

So your first problem was getting enough sucking and cuddling so that you outgrow the need for it too much, too desperately later on. (You're a bit the victim of circumstance here, since you're dependent on parents you are in no position to choose.)

Then you face your second real problem, at the age of nine months or so.

Your first love!

And your first anxiety attack! (Anxiety being dread, fear, worry, total panic, experienced consciously or unconsciously, that haunts us to a greater or lesser degree all our lives from this time on. We are not talking about physical fear, a natural biological intelligence of survival. But of psychological fear, the fear of abandonment, of what might be.)

Until now, a baby hasn't felt itself as separate from its mother. She and everything else is experienced as part of itself. Until now, as long as the baby is fed and cuddled and changed and its little body is happy, it doesn't really care who copes, mother, father, grandmother, helper, or Santa Claus. Its self-worth is in good shape, and it feels protected. It will smile at anyone who happens to be around.

And then, suddenly, the baby becomes a person. It finally sees its mother as separate from itself; and boy or girl, its mother is its first love. Now you cry if your father or your grandmother tries to give you a bottle. You want your mother. Foster children suffer terribly here, without a mother, without consistency. You don't just need love, you love back, you have joined the human race. And in the moment of joining it, you are aware of suffering. If your mother leaves the room, you panic and cry. You don't know yet that she will come back. At that age, babies have no sense of coming and going, nor any sense of time. Later on, you'll play hide-and-seek over and over again to reassure yourself that your mother doesn't disappear over the moon just because you can't see her. But at eight months or nine months, you don't know that yet. You feel what is called separation anxiety. (The feeling will come back to you later when you fall in love in your teens. Absence may bring intense longing, and you'll say or think or write, "I can't live without you.") Adults who haven't outgrown intense separation anxiety will feel the same way they did as babies.

The process of civilization begins with relationship. It's got its joys, but when the elements of attachment, possessiveness, dependency are present, it's got its problems. And with these primitive drives, you need help. It is now that you begin to develop your self to give you a hand. You have discovered that you live in a world of vanishing objects and people. Your self begins to help you learn ways to get them back, especially that most adored person, your mother. You cry. (Later on, you'll learn to be adorable, to get attention, or to be difficult, or do well in school. Right now, you holler.) A mother who knows how to love and nurture will be able to judge those cries. She won't come running every two minutes at the first sound. That could make a baby anxious that it did really need constant protection, that there really was something fearfully wrong. But when the cry sounds distressful, especially at this age in the middle of the night, she will come to soothe and cuddle. And little by little, the baby learns that even if its mother leaves the room, magically she will return.

The other thing that helps separation anxiety is travel. You've begun to crawl around now, to discover the world of tables, chairs, your father's glasses, your brother's baseball. You discover the permanence of many objects, which adds to your sense of security that all things don't disappear forever. You also develop a hunger beyond body hunger, a hunger for the world, curiosity about everything. Your brain-computer has begun to expand. This curiosity is one of the paramount capacities of primates, especially human beings. We search for as much information as we can to download.

Two other things happen of great importance in the next few months.

The beginning of ambivalent feelings, having opposite emotions at the same time. You adore your mother and you can get mad and hate her simultaneously. She has begun to civilize you, wipe your hands and face a lot now that you get dirtier crawling, maybe begun handing you a cup instead of your beloved bottle once in a while, and especially she has begun to use the word NO, which makes you absolutely furious. Why shouldn't you put your father's coin collection piece by piece into your mouth or stick a finger into the electric socket if you feel like it?

And around the age of a year or so, comes the do-it-myself urge, the beginning of a baby's need to master its own environment. My own daughter went on a hunger strike. She who had always been a good eater suddenly wouldn't eat breakfast and then lunch and then dinner. She obviously wasn't sick. She just clamped her mouth shut and pushed my hand away, or if I did get a bit of cereal in her mouth, promptly spat it right in my eye. Finally, in total frustration, I banged the spoon down that evening on her high chair tray. Hannah smiled, picked up the spoon and fed herself dinner, or at least whatever was left after she had poked her fingers into it and smeared it around. I gagged twice at the beautiful face smeared with spinach and smiled back at her happy smile. A major triumph of her need to master her environment over my need to avoid messes, of her expanding capability over my cultural voice that had been telling my brain food messes were yucky. I greeted the emerging person of my lovely, stubborn, independent child.

A baby whose needs for food and touching, for affection and acceptance, for stimulation and attention, aren't met doesn't learn to trust, to bond.

A baby whose mother doesn't cope well with its feelings of abandonment never gets over the feeling that people won't forever desert it.

A baby not allowed to explore the world around it doesn't develop a need to learn, as a baby who isn't talked to doesn't learn to speak.

A baby whose mother doesn't accept its ambivalent feelings with humor and understanding, who feels too threatened or angry or guilty about a baby's attacks, learns to feel guilty itself about negative feelings.

A baby whose mother doesn't help it to get over helplessness may be dependent all its life.

So, with any luck, you've had enough sucking and affection, you've begun to learn to cope with anxiety, you've made a beginning at mastering your life, and your brain is developing enough personal experience to get what you need from the real world. If this is true, you will have outgrown, rather than become stuck in babyhood. You will not be needy and dependent always. As Michael Riera puts it, you're getting ready to establish a consistent and reliable manner of dealing with the world. Or as Erikson says, you will have learned to trust that you and the world are okay.

Only now, the next crisis is at hand.

# *The Potty*

By now, the ratio of your food and hugs has been established, according to your needs or not. During the second and third year of your life, you've got a new shock coming. The potty.

The issue up for grabs here is learning self-control in order to win your parents' love and approval — or sticking to the messes that give you pleasure and losing out on all those happy, clucking noises your mother makes when she tries to make some headway in civilizing you. Here we go with your first real taste of what civilization calls "good" and "bad" behavior. This may have nothing to do with what is morally right or wrong: it is just a message of what your group has decided is acceptable and has relayed to you through your parents.

Psychologists sometimes call this the anal stage, as they called your babyhood the oral stage. The names are obvious, the struggles not always. How you and your mother got through this stage will have an important influence on the formation of your personality, along with, of course, your particular culture's directives about personal habits and parental control. But from outhouses in the South Pacific to the use of sand in the desert, from the use of water in India to Western toilet paper, the struggle to make you conform to the laws of the pack begins.

*When Jim was in his teens, some curious patterns of behavior became obvious. He was extremely neat, clean, and fussy about his room. He had many collections: miniature cars, paperweights, books, toy soldiers, card decks. And everything had to be in a certain place. When he went to sleep at night, if things weren't neatly lined up, if the window was an inch too high or too low, if his blankets weren't exactly arranged, he was too upset to sleep until it was all arranged as he wished. His behavior also took on certain ritual patterns. He had to brush his teeth a certain way, wash his hands just so. And Jim was more than careful with his money, he was stingy. And as he was stingy with money, he was stingy with his emotions. Everything was kept in, and the tight, closed expression of his mouth emphasized his feeling. His attitudes about every issue were conservative, proper, uptight. Jim's was a personality with almost no give.*

Jim's personality is a good example of what can happen to a child who is toilet-trained too early, too severely. It could have been worse. He might also have become a sadist (someone who likes to inflict cruelty) or a masochist (someone who likes to receive cruelty).

This and all the following upbringing practices are not necessarily a question of parental or caregiver fault: sometimes simply the child's own genetic makeup inclines it toward hypersensitivity or an easy-going shrug. What will make one of us weird may not affect others at all.

There are two points to remember about the potty period. A baby experiences a bowel movement as pleasure, not only for itself but as a present to its mother. It seems to make her so happy. When the child is then expected to deposit this treasure in a special place (and also to flush or cover it), the child for the first time understands there is something dirty about this treasure, that it can be used as an insult, an aggressive weapon toward its parents.

If parents push too hard, too early, with too much disapproval for failure to use the potty, the child, during its typical two-year-old struggle for independence anyway, may learn to punish its parents by withholding its bowel movement when it's potty time. This is Jim's story. Defying his mother's need to control him, he withheld what she wanted most when she put him on the toilet. He eventually withheld everything, emotions, money (a child's interest in the treasures its body produces is later on transferred to the treasures of the world—money, collections—and sometimes to a need to produce something of itself, which may help lead later on to the pleasure people take in drawing or writing.)

But not in Jim's case. What he learned to do was punish by holding back. At least he was not beaten for toilet mistakes or other infractions, for abused children abuse others when they grow up. But he did understand that something he did was dirty, so in reaction he grew up cleaner than anyone else. His proper, conservative attitudes are part of this conditioning — no messy edges, everything neat, orderly, and in its place. Jim even counted his possessions, counted his friends, counted his accomplishments, his money continually. Children sometimes feel that bowel movements are part of itself, and become afraid of parts of themselves or their things disappearing, so they count to make certain nothing is missing. It's amazing how much biology can sometimes account for psychology! Eating and elimination have so far accounted for a lot.

Sooner or later, usually between two and three, everybody (unless there is mental retardation or other physical or emotional problems) gets toilet-trained, through fear of loss of affection and approval, and, if they are lucky, in a triumph of self-control instead of tyranny. As Selma Fraiberg says, approving successes and not troubling too much over failures is the way to go.

So, if your parents, if they were aware of your need to rebel, to be independent, to exert some control over your own life and body, had clapped for an appropriate performance, let it go if there were no performance, didn't struggle for the reins to control your little body, your dignity and sense of accomplishment survived intact. Parents sometimes forget what Dorothy Corkille Briggs says in her book *Your Child's Self-Esteem* — "Remember, approval is an oxygen line, particularly for the young child."

It's hard in a rushed world, when both parents work, to pay so much attention to a tiny dignity. But in the long run, parents who give their children a feeling of independence at this stage, not just with the potty, but which shirt to wear or what food to eat first, even at this young age, may not have to cope with teenagers who have to rebel all over again to assert themselves.

A lot of those angry, rebellious feelings you have now as a teenager — the need to control your own life, the fear that you'll never get out from under your parents — have their origin in your second and third year. It is a stage you won't remember, of course, consciously anyway, because you didn't have enough words. Words are the fixatives of conscious memory.

The age of a year-and-a-half to three years is also the age of magical thinking; a belief is born that will last all your life that wishes can cause events. A baby wants its bottle. Magically, it appears. A baby wants a hug. Hopefully that too magically appears. As language develops, and therefore the ability to form and communicate abstract ideas, the small magician learns about causes and events. Except that always in some secret part of the mind, it still believes in wishes. A three-year-old is angry at daddy for being firm about bedtime. Or for not being there at bedtime, or ever, if there is divorce or abandonment. If soon after, daddy breaks his arm, doesn't show up, goes to jail, dies, the child may well believe it was due to its own bad wishes for daddy. If a child wishes, hopes, and nags everybody in sight for a teddy bear for Christmas and gets it, the child may still believe it was magic. Rituals come from magical thinking. (You know the kind — if I pray for a thing standing on my head, I'll get it, or if I don't think about it, it will happen, or if I check under the bed three times, I'll be safe from the horrible hand that reaches out and grabs feet.)

Repeated ritual wards off fears of the unknown and anxieties over the feared. The second, third, and fourth years are full of these fears and anxieties.

Separateness is all very well, but now that you know you are separate from your mother, she may desert you at any time! At that stage, you also crave independence, which makes for conflicting behavior: you're awful all day, and then you get hysterical if your mother goes out for the evening. You're fine about your working mother leaving you at daycare twelve mornings in a row, and on the thirteenth you're furious. (Teenagers go through this conflict intensely again, the need for independence and the need for caring.)

The world is fascinating and you want to be out there, but there are objects, sounds, and sudden movements — like somebody else at daycare or in the street whacking you on the head — that are positively fearful, even painful.

You love your father, but after he's said, "Don't touch my scotch," six times — and on the sixth round his voice is a mite explosive, you may be afraid of him. Or you may displace your fear onto the monster on television you were never afraid of before.

You took a bath nicely until you were three, played with your duckies, and enjoyed yourself thoroughly. One day you refuse to get into the tub. And the next day. And the next, screaming like a banshee. Your mother may or may not figure out you are terrified of going down the bathtub drain like the water. You aren't exactly scientific yet about the sizes of things.

Or the reasons for sizes. A three-year-old friend of mine went through a period of stuffing herself on the grounds that if you ate a lot you got fat and had a baby.

Back to anxiety. Children cope with it primarily through repetitive play and words, if they are healthy.

*My son Danny was never a sleeper. Before he was born, I read Dr. Spock from cover to cover and noted happily how many hours of the day babies and young children slept. I got an oddball. Not only did he sleep less than any other known creature of his age and size, but when he hit the age of three, balked at going to bed at all. Why miss out on whatever fun was coming up next? It was painful for Danny, separating himself from his beloved world. I spent a lot of time reading stories to him, his father chatted with him when I grew hoarse. And then, Danny hit upon a method all his own. One night he began to talk himself to sleep. In rhythmical, musical cadences sort of like rap I could hear him discussing the day's events to himself, in singsong tones. "Went out to play today, had a very good time...played with Neddie, ate my lunch, drew a picture for mommy...." And on and on and on until he fell asleep. The habit went on for a long time and eventually came to include commentaries on Sesame Street and the state of the world he had heard about on the six o'clock news.*

This is the pleasure of language. With words, Danny could recapture his world and comfort himself in the dark. And the repetition of any fears he had had lessened their impact. It also clued his parents about Danny's inner world— they admit to have eavesdropped on occasion!

Repetition is a major way to relieve anxiety by mastering something over and over again. You have all this developing ability to understand the rites and rituals and expectations of your particular society's corner of the world through the open and the hidden agenda of the people who take care of you (as they tell you what to do and what not to do over and over and over and over again).

You have the force of the outside world thrusting in on you, through television, books, video, music, movies, in the street, on your block, in your project, your town, your neighborhood. And you have this new sense of being a person separate from others that nobody tells you how to handle. With all of this, comes the dawn of a new idea.

And, naturally, the next shock to the system.

# Will You Marry Me, Mommy, Daddy?

Sex.
Many people are horrified to discover that young children have a sex life, that infantile sexuality not only exists but that the way in which this stage is resolved determines the child's future ability to form healthy relationships either with the opposite sex or their own sex or whatever their gender preference. It can be the make or break stage. And an

awful lot of people don't make it, and almost nobody makes it all the way. This is a third example of biology as well as environment, nature as well as nurture, influencing psychology.

Infantile sexuality continues to embarrass parents.

Only what could be more natural?

Consider!

The child has growing powers of observation. To the child's sense of separateness from its parents comes a sense of something between its parents the child doesn't understand — that has nothing to do with the child, that leaves the child out. Nighttime noises, maybe even investigated, maybe something seen or heard. (Never underestimate the curiosity of a child.) What is happening?

The child is curious about itself, its own sensations, touch, smells, all its body sensations. Children have, of course, touched their genitals before, but around the age of four, they attach particular pleasure to fondling themselves. Not much happens when they masturbate at this age because they aren't physically mature, but their bodies do respond pleasurably.

Which makes them wonder about other bodies. And the combination of pleasure and curiosity makes them go find out if they can. It depends on the relative state of home dress or undress, tropical versus arctic climates that cause people to dress in a loosely-draped cloth or nose-to-toes wrappings. It depends on the availability of brothers and sisters, neighborhood friends, nursery-school going-to-the-bathroom procedures. Whatever, children discover.

BOYS AND GIRLS! THE DIFFERENCE!

Why? What for?

Boys have a penis, girls have a vagina. Both are quick to understand, not only that there is a difference, but that the difference matters. Freud was wrong when he said girls envy the possession of a penis. Girls don't want penises any more than boys want uteruses. What girls envy is a boy's freedom. What girls envy is that societies all over the world prefer boys and have a tendency to let little girls die by leaving them in ditches or under rocks in China and India, by making them second-class citizens in Europe, Japan, and the United States, by genitally mutilating them in Africa, by covering their faces, hiding them without legal rights in many Near East countries, by prostituting girls or bartering them in marriage, by giving boys rights over girls everywhere.

Most psychologists now understand that both sexes are capable of envying each other. Girls envy the freedom and special treatment given boys, and boys as men may eventually experience envy of women's ability to produce babies, perhaps even envy women's freedom to express emotion.

It must be remembered how long ago Freud lived. Female psychology was not really possible for him, and basically he was your average male chauvinist. Not to take away from the genius of his discoveries about the unconscious of human beings in general, but he was just a little short of information about women and did a lot of damage with what misinformation he produced. Feminist psychologists and writers in this century like Mary Pipher in her 1994 *Reviving*

*Ophelia: Saving the Selves of Adolescent Girls*; *SchoolGirls: Young Women, Self-Esteem, and the Confidence Gap* by Peggy Orenstein, 1993; *Girls Are Equal Too*, 1998, by Dale Carlson, and works by Betty Friedan, Gloria Steinem, Karen Horney, Carolyn Heilbrun, Naomi Wolf's *Beauty Myth*, and others will offer more accurate views of female psychology.

Most developmental and sociological psychology books have been written for males by males. A good new one is *Boys to Men, Maps for the Journey* by Greg Alan Williams.

*Joining the Tribe: Growing Up Gay & Lesbian in the '90's* by Linnea Due describes the hardships from stigmatism of sexual minority youth, the challenges faced by our gay, lesbian, bisexual, and transgender children.

Mike Riera's *Surviving High School* is a good handbook for navigating the hazards of teenage life, including friendships, sex, drugs, driving, family, divorce, and suicide. Farai Chideya's *Don't Believe the Hype: Fighting Cultural Misinformation About African-Americans* mirrors another variety of teenage experience.

I mention these books here because while there's a reading list at the back of this book, not everybody will go there. But do read, because as W.E.B. Du Bois describes in *The Souls of Black Folk*, it isn't much fun, "...this sense of always looking at one's self through the eyes of others, of measuring one's soul by the tape of a world that looks on in amused contempt and pity." It's even worse, if you belong to a minority like people of color, people with disabilities, gays and lesbians, or teenagers in general, or to a group of people who have consistently been treated as if they were second-class, like females, always to be reading about yourselves through the eyes of those temporarily in power.

But back to the major divisions among us, boys and girls.

The important point here to parents and future parents is to catch the beginning of this childhood sexuality stage in time (you'll get hints from your child's questions if you don't actually see any of its experiences) and tell your little girl that she has something important inside her body, hidden for protection, that she can't see, just as a little boy has something important that's visible.

A nd speaking of questions, this is the age for the question. Where do I come from? Where do babies come from? And, in whatever terminology, how does all this equipment work?

The combination of discovering that its parents have a special relationship and discovering the differences or at least really for the first time experiencing the differences in their bodies makes children suddenly very aware of MALE AND FEMALE, and with their strong and passionate attachments within the family — who belongs to who and who doesn't.

While it is true that ancient Egyptian royalty married brothers and sisters to keep the throne in the family, and there are countries where first cousins are permitted to marry, most of society for thousands of years has placed a TABOO on INCEST, sex between brothers and sisters and first cousins, but especially parents and children.

Four-year-olds don't know this.

## Boys

*At four, Georgie knows he's a boy, he feels sexual but even stronger emotional yearnings, and since his mother is the woman he loves most, he quite naturally "falls in love" with his mother. He will become at this stage an adorer, a "mommy's boy." Georgie will, depending on his temperament, propose once or quite regularly. "When I grow up, I'm going to marry you, Mommy, right?" There is obviously, one slight problem. Daddy. At the moment, clearly it is daddy who is married to mommy. And this is the crux. On the one hand, Georgie loves his daddy. On the other, daddy has to be disposed of if Georgie is going to get mommy. His panicky conflict can be awesome. To say nothing of what will happen to Georgie, being small, if daddy, being big, should find out how Georgie feels. Georgie knows what will happen. Daddy will take away what Georgie has now learned to value most, his manhood, his penis. So in that small person of Georgie, the little, happy-go-lucky, carefree creature digging away in his sandbox or riding his tricycle down the sidewalk, there is a raging conflict of love, murder, and terror.*

Under normal circumstances, if Georgie's feelings are understood and well-handled, Georgie's mother will accept his love with affection and humor (no seduction to encourage his sexual attachment to her and ruin him for other women), and Georgie's father will understand his son's temporary ambivalence of hero-worship on the one hand and murderous jealousy on the other. He will know that Georgie is not going to spend his life in her pocket just because for the time being he hangs around his mother a lot. He will outgrow this stage as reality forces him to understand that he can't have his mother. Not only will his father (or if there is no father, other males or society in general) zip him into a body bag if he tries, but Georgie's very real love for his father will help him to identify with his father male to male. Georgie is then no longer a mommy's boy. He becomes a man like his father. He's going to have a lot of bad dreams through this period (often in the form of being chased by a big, bad, scary animal — daddy, naturally), but when he emerges at around six years old from this most difficult conflict, his life will be a lot smoother. The civilizing, restrictive, instructional voices of his parents and society are now internalized. Georgie's head has now developed echoing voices that tell him what is expected of him. The father's role in helping his son through this stage is not usually stressed enough. If the fathers shows too much disapproval or even contempt for this mommy's boy stage, the boy may experience so much rejection that it makes it difficult for him to identify properly with his father. Boys need their father's love and support to become adequate men. In our society men often withhold emotion from their sons, come down on them too hard, make them roughen up, toughen up too fast. Sons then compensate in some other way for the loss of fatherly love.

With girls, this stage comes a little later and can be more problematical because there is no fear of castration to end parental passion with such finality. Many men, but many more women, go through life without ever having resolved the longing for their fathers in one form or another.

*That, of course, is the biggest problem of this period when you first discover your own sexuality and your attachment to your parents. If it isn't outgrown properly — you can be psychologically stuck with the problem of never getting over being hung up on your parents, negatively if you didn't like them, positively if you did.*

## Girls

*Just like Georgie, Mary's first love is also her mother. This makes things a little more complicated for Mary than for Georgie, because Mary will not only have to change love-objects during this early sexualized period, she will also have to cope harder later on with resolving her feelings for her own sex. In early adolescence, girls form closer, more intense friendships and relationships with other girls than boys do with boys, reliving and resolving their childhood attachments to their mothers.*

*Marry me, Daddy, comes up for a girl around six, not four. Mary, who until then, may have been mommy's darling, will suddenly shock mommy by rejecting her, by being jealous and possessive and competitive about daddy. It is Mary who understands daddy better than mommy does, it is Mary whom daddy truly loves. And since most daddies bask in this terrific adoration, a secret part of Mary will go through life believing daddy basically preferred her, and if it weren't for the generation gap, etc. But Mary is in for the same shock as Georgie. She can't have daddy all to herself. Only here there is a difference. There isn't the terrible castration/death fear to end her feelings, and the result is that unlike Georgie, Mary's sexual feelings are not so completely buried for the next few years. She will be ready for boys, new love objects to replace daddy, earlier in her teens than Georgie will be ready for girls. She will not only be less repressed than Georgie, she will be more open to relationships with boys because there were no earlier fears attached to loving someone of the opposite sex. Besides, girls are allowed to show their feelings more openly. Anyway, Mary will give up the idea of marrying daddy the same way Georgie gave up mommy, and she will begin to identify with mommy so she can later get someone like daddy for herself.*

## Gays and Lesbians

Ten percent of all children everywhere, Asian children, European children, African children, Hispanic children, American children, Australian children are gay and lesbian, same-sex instead of opposite-sex oriented. Another word for this same-sex orientation is homosexuality. This is rarely due to environment, conditioning, early training, even sexual molestation. **Most important to understand, this is not a matter of choice.** Who would choose to be so persecuted, stigmatized, made less than, hounded into suicide, the streets — who would choose to be so lonely, so lost, when among other minority groups at least you've got your family with you and if you're gay or lesbian you're all by yourself even in your family. Babies born gay become children who are gay become teenagers who are gay become gay adults. This is no more unusual in the human race than having blue eyes. Why do we drive ourselves and them nuts over this?

## Conscience or Cultural Voices

In *The Magic Years*, Selma Fraiberg describes the conscience as the "repository of moral values, of ideals and standards for behavior…not effective if it reigns as a tyrant within the ego, mercilessly forbidding and tormenting or accusing and punishing for the smallest transgressions."

The reason I like that description is that so many consciences are killers, cripplers, assassins, Nazi police, not only of the self, but of others. It is in these years you can be taught to love, to hate, to separate yourself out from or be part of everyone else, to put yourself above or below other national, sexual, religious, ethnic groups of people. You can be taught these things as quickly and easily as how to give up your bottle, potty yourself in private, or not to marry your mother.

If all goes well, a child outgrows its early childhood to go on to bigger and better things. If not, if parents use their power to make a child feel guilty and terrible about itself and its feelings, it will go on carrying those feelings and the child will feel guilty and terrible about itself for life. Without maybe ever knowing why. A well-constructed conscience is a marvelous tool for self-discipline (do your homework and get some approval, dear), for creating an appropriate amount of guilt (it's not nice to break someone's knees, dear), for keeping yourself reasonably clean, orderly, well-mannered so you don't run amuck. A cruel, tyrannical conscience that comes from parents who overuse their power to control you, gives you the feeling you're too awful to love and be loved. With little or no development of the conscience, you could become a criminal. With too much, nothing you ever do, no relationship you ever form, will be right. Everything will be guilt-ridden.

And beyond how you learned to judge yourself, how righteous and judgmental was the cultural voice of your conscience taught to be about others?

Play a game.

Get a piece of paper and a pencil and write down some of the messages in your brain, recorded there from childhood. See if you really accept them as truths, or are they just messages relayed to you about the views necessary to hold if you want protection from the herd you were born in to. At least know the difference between your recorded messages and what is really right.

Finish these sentences and see what you've been told. Do you really agree? Really?

Jocks are ............................................................................

Gay people are ...................................................................

Black people are .................................................................

White people are ................................................................

Girls are ...............................................................................

Parents are...........................................................................

Kids are.................................................................................

People with disabilities are .............................................

The Chinese are ..................................................................

Smart people are ...............................................................

If something you've been taught turns out to be wrong, you know, you can just say to your voices and your selves, "Don't go there."

Not only the voices of the conscience, the cultural agenda, but those of the personal agenda are strongly affected during this three-ish to six-ish period. Erik Erikson and other ego analysts have stressed the importance of the emerging personal identity of a child — whether it is helped to grow by parents' recognition of a child's real accomplishment (of an achievement that has real meaning in our culture — anything from learning to walk to buttoning a jacket) or whether its achievements are ignored or overly criticized. A child's sense of worth, not only in terms of accomplishments but feelings, needs to be guarded carefully during these years.

It's a matter basically of a child's being told all along that it is okay, its feelings are okay, having as many anxieties as possible ironed out, or at least being helped to handle them.

Take the difference between:

"Johnny, you're a bad boy," and "Johnny, you're an incredible kid, but I'm not too crazy about mopping up a quart of Kool-Aid or untangling the guinea pig from your sister's hair."

Seems like a small difference in words. It isn't.

Especially not at this stage, when the kid may feel "bad" enough. The difference is in bringing up a child to feel that even if some of the things he or she does are a touch out of line, basically he or she is a wonderful, okay person and will sooner or later learn to put his or her shoes on the right feet. A child should come to understand that its needs are acceptable, even if those needs can't always be met, that its feelings are valid even if some of the outlets (smashing glasses against the wall in a rage) aren't.

During childhood, a child learns to value itself according to how its parents value it. It values other people according to how its parents value them, god and the universe, animals and trees.

It will also feel about others the way it feels about itself.

If a child is made to feel that its bowel movement is messy, the child will end up feeling that she or he is messy and dirty and so is everybody else.

If a child is found masturbating or asks questions about sex or its own body and is met with embarrassment, disapproval, disgust, those are the feelings the child will feel about its own sexuality and everybody else's when it grows up.

If a child isn't given the right to feel — love, anger, rage, sadness, joy, passion (and make no mistake, the feelings of children are just as powerful only a hundred times more confused than adults') — the feelings twist and go underground. They don't go away. They just bide their time and torture the child in the adult it becomes and everyone else in its path.

If a child's passionate attachment to its parents, its need for their love and approval, isn't met, a child may spend its life wandering and looking for that same love and approval without ever being satisfied.

We cannot function with any degree of mental health if our basic needs haven't been met, our contact with reality — our own and others' — isn't solid, or our consciences are merciless. Biological, personal, cultural voices must be healthy and understood.

The bad news is, almost nobody has completely healthy voices.

The good news is, if you pay attention to understanding your voices (this is a kind of meditation, this attention) you can change your behavior and do what's right, no matter what your voices say. Shut up and let me rethink this, is a good beginning.

If your parents haven't loved you properly, you'll have to teach yourself. Unlike Forrest Gump, most people don't know what loving is. This is because parents are usually more concerned with teaching you to fit in and be safe than right living. Living rightly is based on what's good for everybody, not just you and your group, and often this requires you to stick your neck out and even sometimes hang by it for a while. But if your parents haven't been able to love you properly, and teach you what loving is and isn't, you'll have to learn for yourself. You can learn to outgrow your need for your parents. You can be free to find new lives. But if you have only learned control and possession, not to love, you'll go on looking for new mommies and daddies and never have a satisfying man-woman relationship, or a man-man relationship, or a woman-woman relationship, or any true relationship at all. You will live and relive with each new person the original ones in a kind of repetition compulsion, and recreate the original fantasy without ever seeing people as they really are.

To grow up healthy in the head, you have to outgrow, not become fixated at, each of these crucial stages of childhood when so much of your personality was formed. You'll find this true for the rest of your life. If you live in the past, see every moment through the eyes of the past, you'll never live at all. Teach yourself to see with new eyes whatever happens, whoever happens to you. And consider that love is a state of being, not a state of attachment.

In case you were wondering, the nicest answer to the question, "Will you marry me, Mommy, Daddy?" is:

"Darling, I think you are the most wonderful Georgie-Mary who ever lived and I love you very much. Only you see I'm already married. But one day you will grow up and find a person to love and marry all on your own."

Reality time. A hard blow for a child. But softened with love, respect, and enthusiasm for things yet to be.

# Underground

From about six years old to ten is repression time, the time for the pushing underground into the unconscious, all those primal and dependency needs. It is the time when a child's sexual energy is sublimated into new paths.

It's not that sexual activity (at this stage, masturbation, exhibitionism, toilet and sex jokes, peeking) goes away. But no new sexual activity happens and no new objects of adoration are looked for. It's been called the latency stage. Latent, meaning to lie hidden, to lurk.

There are other energies and motives besides sexual drives, of course: the energy for doing, for mastering the environment, for exploring, for learning, for life itself.

This is the stage when the emphasis changes from the basic drives to the growing control of conscious life: daily activities; school; sports; friendships; whatever is cool for your group to do. There is an eager interest in the outer world and mastering it instead of concentrating on one's own insides and conflicts. The passion once directed toward mommy and daddy is repressed, and is expressed through the process of sublimation — using your energy for other things, for more socially acceptable outlets such as artistic, intellectual, athletic, humanistic activities.

This is where the evil of comparison emerges. This is when, instead of being watered so whatever you are can bloom, you are given comparative marks at school, given comparative estimates of what you are or should be (you're faster than your brother, not as smart as your mother, prettier than your sister, not as nice as your cousin, better than your friends, worse than your friends, and on and on and on). This makes you mad, hurts your feelings, makes you ambitious enough to step on other people's necks, makes you so insecure you nurture plans for living under a bed.

There is intense sibling rivalry, competition for parents' attention among brothers and sisters, constant fighting and yelling and pushing for attention in school, from friends and teachers. In the wild, animals establish pecking orders at this stage. So do human beings. There is fierce competition for favor from parents, for preference in school. And if positive attention seems impossible to attain, negative attention will do. It's the beginning of if-I-can't-get-first-prize-I'd-rather-get-hung-on-a-nail-than-get-no-attention-at-all. This is the point where if children don't have a healthy sense of worth and confidence, they can practically destroy one another's personal sense of esteem. This is a marvelous time to tell children that it's important to do their best without killing the competition. The struggle to master their environment is also a marvelous outlet for the anger they don't dare risk using against parents or friends for fear of losing approval. Such physical and emotional avenues of escape are necessary now.

Because all that psychic energy will out. All the passion you had for your parents, all the passion you have for life, all that life force, has to go somewhere. An interesting result of all this frantic activity during the latency period when school, friends, and activities become important releases for all that energy is the wonderful discovery that there are other sources for approval besides mommy and daddy. Peter Blos in his book *On Adolescence* says:

> *The dependency on parental assurance for feelings of worth and significance is progressively replaced during the latency period by a sense of self-esteem derived from achievements and mastery which earn objective and social approbation.*

Meaning, that's cool, if my old man doesn't like me, I still got that A in spelling so something about me must be okay. It's the age at which not everything depends on looking in the parent-mirror for approval. You discover you can get approval from other people. Even more important, you discover you feed yourself with your own approval; that if you do something well, you can break your arm patting your own back.

You will have noticed that the ego defense mechanisms discussed in Section I are really developing now. You are coping with anxieties, disturbing memories (who wants to remember a lot of the stuff you had to go through during your babyhood, the painful shocks of early childhood), sexual drives (you really aren't ready for that yet), anger (don't forget anger — it will make you furious forever that you couldn't have everything you wanted when you were little), and all the other unpleasant numbers in your unconscious. You cope by denial (I just won't acknowledge the painful feeling), by repression (stuffing the gross thoughts underground), projection (you're angry, I'm not), displacement (I love my teacher, not my mother; I'll kick the wall, not my best friend), conversion (it's not that I don't want to go to school, I just have a pain in my left ear), sublimation, and all the others.

These defenses seem to occur in immature nervous systems and brains too young for clarity and insight, or in young lives where the time is not taken to explain or talk over human nature. So the brain uses these mechanisms to protect the conscious self from overloading.

## Neglect and Abuse

Neglected children from Eastern European orphanages where infants are often simply warehoused, untouched, unnurtured, only fed and clothed, have taught us a great deal about the actual physical effect on the brain of abusive neglect. Adopting American couples in partnership with psychiatric centers, psychologists, social workers, have had to learn the causes for the disruptive behavior of neglected infancy and childhood. What they have learned applies to children around the world in the same circumstances: our own homeless children, children who grow up imprisoned in projects because of street violence, children who are abused right in their own middle and upper class homes.

Not all, but many of the 10,000 babies adopted from Eastern European countries like Russia and Romania were warehoused. Their lack of love, attention, stimulation in the first years has resulted in actually visible brain damage when CAT scans show the pictures of their brains. Because of this deprivation, they suffer developmental delays and disorders in attention, language, and particularly in their inability to form attachments to anybody; to respond to affection, to care. In brains starved in early stages when emotional needs are not met, they are unable to connect to parents, they lash out with biting, screaming, cruelty to animals, other children, they can be hypersensitive to touch, to sound, taste, hearing, and their brains do not process information and stimuli as quickly as other children so it is difficult for them to keep up in school.

What this tells us about our brains is that personal experience literally, physically changes our brain chemistry. The good news is that much damage can be reversed. We have discovered that in many cases holding therapy helps the hypersensitivity to touch. Holding therapy consists of giving the child the hours of hugs and stroking missed in infancy. We have discovered that speaking repetitively and slowly — just as we talk to babies, who then repeat sounds and give their brains feedback over and over again to create the simple building blocks of language — can reverse the damage of abused, neglected, traumatized brains and repair and retrain the damaged centers. What we learn generally about ourselves from the exaggerated problems of neglected children is that all of our brains have been to some extent neglected, and the good news is — we can observe and repair damage with attention and affection.

## Genes

Just as experience and learning actually modify the chemicals of the brain, so do genetic factors. Behavioral biologists tell us there are personality-forming genes you have inherited from your family that affect you as well as nurture or lack of it, personal experience, the racial repository in your unconscious, society's voices through parents, peers, media. By race, we mean the *human* race: it's the only one there is.

Some stuff you may simply inherit, like a quick temper, the result of adrenaline rushes you inherit from your Aunt Martha. You may simply copy her behavior, of course, but brain chemicals, hormones, genes and the DNA they contain interact with your environment and upbringing to form not only your behavior but your moods, your capacity for happiness or depression, your tendencies to be overanxious or fearful, daring or enthusiastic. Your personality and even your capacities are the results of biological inheritance as well as your nurturing. Like a talent for music, a patient disposition, the knock knees that make you a reader instead of a track star, your ability to survive your own disasters — all this may be in your genetic coding.

Yet — environment and the people around you can also change the brain chemicals! The brain chemistry and nerve cells are not set in cement. They alter and reorganize the brain — and you — all your life. Change your behavior, and you actually change your physical brain! *You are not stuck with either how you were born, nor how you were brought up.*

## You and the World

The time of about six years to ten is when you get to see if everything you have so far collected in your personality is enough to survive with in the world. The growth of confidence in mastering the outer world is very important during this period. Because with the hurricane of adolescence, confidence will weaken again under the onslaught of violently demanding basic drives.

Before you can have a halfway decent adolescence, you have to have achieved a few things psychologically during the breather from sexual turmoil that comes at this stage. You have to have learned to use your intellect properly, to have developed judgment, understood the general rules of society, and especially sympathy and compassion for other people. You also have to have learned to measure yourself to some extent, to avoid the extremes of inferiority or superiority to everyone else. If all goes well, you achieve the right physical size and shape. And you develop confidence to cope with anxiety and not fall apart under normal stress so you don't crack up or have to go running to your parents all the time for help and reassurance. And you can say, "Good for you, baby," without needing someone else to stick a gold star on your forehead.

At least you better hope all this has happened. Because puberty is upon you.

*Section Three*

---

# EARLY
# ADOLESCENCE

# *I'm Not Interested—Yet*

Somewhere around the age of ten, eleven, twelve, in some cultures as early as eight, in some as late as fourteen, nature is going to play an interesting trick on you. The name of the trick is puberty.

### Bodies

You're hardly an adult. You're not even an adolescent, emotionally. But like it or not — and a lot don't — biologically speaking, your body, if not your head is getting ready to grow up. This throws quite a kink into your physical, emotional, and mental machinery.

For the past three or four years, you've been pretty free of strong sexual drives. You've been concentrating on mastering the world (whether that world is about skipping down a small-town hill or trying to stay alive in the inner city streets), measuring yourself, trying to figure out if you're inferior or superior (the great trial of the past stage) to everybody else. And now, all of a sudden, your maturing body reawakens the needs of your sexual nature. And with that reawakening, you will have to relive and re-resolve all those earlier conflicts of your childhood before you can reach psychological maturity.

But before you begin to resolve those conflicts, most especially to outgrow your emotional dependency on your parents in order to form new attachments, you first have to cope with the shock of your changing body and its needs.

From here on, everybody worries about physical appearance. Am I tall enough (boys); am I too tall (every boy is smaller than me at school); am I too fat; are my breasts going to be big enough (or will I ever get them at all—and the size comparison goes for boys, too, concerning their genitals); are my hair texture and skin color all right; am I wearing the right clothes; am I clueless about the newest moves; and so forth. The interest in being thin, the eating disorders anorexia and bulimia — starving so you don't eat at all or throwing up what you do eat — from this time on is part of what Mary Pipher calls our girl-poisoning culture in her 1994 book *Reviving Ophelia: Saving the Selves of Adolescent Girls.* The extra concerns of girls about their appearance are also well discussed in *SchoolGirls: Young Women, Self-Esteem, and the Confidence Gap* by Peggy Orenstein based on the *AAUW Report How Schools Shortchange Girls.* What the concern with appearance does when it is carried to extremes is affect your confidence, your ability to perform, in our society where appearances are too important. Looks can get you accepted or rejected too quickly as a sex partner, even as a friend.

Along with physical appearance, from here on, other body stuff worries everybody. Everybody worries about masturbation, sexual fantasies. Among boys, there are worries about erections at unexpected times and having orgasms while they sleep. Girls worry about menstruation and knowing they can get pregnant. In our society, sexual activity has begun earlier and earlier. Planned Parenthood facilities report younger and younger girls coming in, and teenage pregnancy, as everybody knows, is more evident. But even among groups where early adolescent children do not yet engage in sex play with one another, they will say "I'm not interested yet." Note the yet. The interest is there. And because of society's taboos in our culture about too-early mating, everybody feels more or less guilty about it all. It is particularly difficult for girls now. A hundred years ago, menstruation did not usually begin until sixteen years of age. Now girls menstruate earlier, at ten or eleven or twelve. This brings about concerns with sexuality even earlier than ever.

This is not true in all societies, but in our society the guilt is built in. Babies are not allowed to play with themselves in public as they are in Samoa. (See Margaret Mead's studies.) The sexual drives toward parents are put down during early childhood, often with no humor and no understanding as in other cultures. And despite all the pornography around, from bookstores to video to the Internet, or maybe even because of it, kids are definitely given the idea, no matter how freely they've been brought up, that sex before you're "grown up" (and in some sad cases even then) is bad. Unfortunately, the taboos extend even to relieving your tensions in our culture. Masturbating is both healthy and perfectly normal and only the guilt over it can hurt you in any way.

Okay. How does all this guilt and tension get handled?

A lot of the angry guilt and sexual tension gets handled by forming gangs, especially by boys. Shared feelings are easier to cope with. Running with a pack of other kids you can identify with, compare lives with, unloose all that pent-up sexual and aggressive energy with, helps a lot. Gangs can be formed to protect turf, attack other gangs, for criminal activity from drug dealing to larceny, or for a healthy game of basketball, scout camping, helping the homeless, serving in soup kitchens.

There are other tensional outlets to ward off anxiety. Compulsive activities can work.

Steve collects rubber bands. He can't pass a desk, a stationary shelf, or overlook a package without checking for rubber bands. Sharon lives in a stable, riding horses or mucking out or mending tack every hour she's not in school.

Damon plays his guitar unless he's asleep. Cheryl plays baseball with a vengeance. It's not just a physical activity, which helps as a tensional outlet, it's an obsession with her. She lives, talks, and breathes baseball. Since the sex drive — with little sexual outlet — is strong at this stage, the single-minded concentration on collections, sports, music, whatever the chosen activity, is equally strong. It's a good defense against instinctual demands.

At this stage, practically anything will do to relieve the tension and anxiety. Gesell describes nail biting, frequent stomach and headaches, strong lip movements, stuttering, muttering, constant hand-to-mouth gestures, fiddling, twitching, hair twirling, even thumb sucking.

But not all the defenses work all of the time, and there may be a lot of fears, just in passing, of the dark, or of planes or whatever, that are displaced fears of a child's own sexuality.

Since the conscience disapproves of the instincts at this point, there is another way girls and boys cope with the conflict between the sexes. Often, they simply avoid each other, especially boys who are still afraid of being castrated for misdemeanor. Girls play with girls now, and boys play with boys. Everybody hates everybody (though they tease and show off for each other) because they have been trained to fear the consequences of being together. (Strange, how after teaching children that the opposite sex is the enemy, we then expect them to grow up, get married to each other, and live happily ever after!)

They also envy each other. Girls go through a period of wishing they had the kind of freedom, muscular power, and society's preferential treatment, that males have. And boys make a lot of things — models, wood structures, whatever — because they envy girls their ability to make babies. Making things allows boys to produce something the way the bodies of girls can, and this drive, if it is strong enough, is part of what produces, in men, great works of art, books, the need to grow things, create businesses, and so forth. Girls have a need to produce these things too, but they also, most of them, have the built-in satisfaction of having babies.

## Parents

Along with developing bodies and sex drives, getting over parents is the major problem of preadolescence.

*Judy is twelve. Like all girls her age, she is reliving and has to resolve her early attachment for her mother. Like all babies, Judy's first love object was mommy. But to grow up, to be independent, to be able to love a boy eventually, she has to struggle against her deep feelings (either love or hate or both) for her mother. To escape her passion for her mother, Judy transfers a lot of those feelings to girl friends. More than anything else, Judy wants two things. She wants a close, intense relationship with one girlfriend who returns her love, loyalty, and approval. And she wants to be very popular in general with a group of girls. She wants admiration from boys, but her greatest interest now is in relationships to girls. Transferring her feelings to other girls is the first step out from under her mother on the way to future adult relationships. Rebelling against mother also helps, and there may be a lot of in-fighting about hairstyles, clothes, chores, anything, to prove or at least test out Judy's breaking-away. If Judy's mother understands what Judy is doing, there need be no permanent rift in their relationship. Judy adores her mother too much — not too little. She needs her mother too much— not too little. If Judy's mother understands what they are going through together — letting go of Judy's babyhood — Judy will then be ready at the proper time and with the appropriate ability to have relationships to friends and to boyfriends and others outside the family.*

*If Judy's mother doesn't understand Judy's strong feelings and her rebellion, if her parents think like so many parents do that their children don't need them enough when the real trouble is children need them too much even if they behave negatively in reaction to those needs, there will be big problems. Rejecting parents can produce a child with frantic feelings. Judy might then have too desperate a need for love, and since she can't get it at home, anger and need will drive her elsewhere. Her behavior at home will be terrible, out of anger, and her need for attachment of some kind will get her into trouble. At this age, girls have as strong sexual desires often as boys, and Judy may confuse sex and love as so many do. The wrong boys, older boys, early pregnancy, indifference to schoolwork, girl gang life — all these may result.*

Boys go through a similar battle. Only boys have two problems to fight in relationship to their mothers. Adolescence really is a state of constant, chronic confusion!

*Charlie, during preadolescence, first has to cope with his earliest passive feelings — being loved, being fed, being done for — and give up as much as possible the receiving role so that he can actively do instead of being done for. Males, in our society, are programmed for and admired for the aggressive, not the passive, role. Charlie's preoccupation with the satisfactions of infancy and the potty period (he may experiment with drinking, his language and jokes may reflect his immature preoccupation with the toilet) express his reliving earlier stages. But the most important battle for Charlie is overcoming the fear of females, of the idea that his mother and other women can unman him. This is the central problem of Charlie's preadolescence, and he will fight it by keeping clear of girls. He will stick with other boys, often have older male heroes. Charlie's struggle to escape his powerful need for his mother will be helped enormously if he has done well during the previous stage and pretty well mastered his environment, gained skills and confidence in his abilities.*

The major difference in everybody's rush to get away from mother during preadolescence, is that girls have a harder time of it than boys. There are a couple of reasons for this.

Society permits far more freedom to boys than girls. Not just physical freedom to explore neighborhoods, streets, the physical world, and experiment sexually, but psychological freedom to achieve, do, be, explore and exploit whatever they wish. They are society's star gender. Girls are taught not to achieve for their own sense of approval, but to win approval from others, such as parents, teachers, boys — by being docile, obedient, passive, not too brainy — and, of course, pretty and, in our movie-star culture, THIN! None of this contributes to independence in thinking or behavior or an ability to break away from home.

The second reason girls have a harder time getting away from mother than boys is more psychologically-sexually complex. A boy doesn't have to change the sex of his love object — it has always been female. He'll just find another female. A girl not only has to transfer her feelings from her first love object, her mother, but switch to someone of the opposite sex. (This is less difficult for lesbians, harder for gay boys.)

Another result of reprocessing all these earlier needs is the growing need for group acceptance, POPULARITY. To replace the earlier sense of security derived from our parents, apparently the entire world has to love us! Anyway, no parents, however terrific, can ever give a child all the adoration and attention it wants or thinks it deserves. Basic drives and needs can be a bottomless pit.

It dawns on the psyche that parents are not going to provide endlessly all the emotions required, and that the remaining attention and love needed must come from the world at large. Skills get attention. Being popular gets what we call love. Everybody envies popular people. Everybody wants to be a rock star. But remember that a lot of popular people — the football hero, the girl with fifteen dates lined up, the boy who remembers the name of everybody he ever met — may be overcompensating (making up for) the disappointment of rejection or neglect at home. Meaning, if you're not as popular as you'd like to be, your psyche just may not feel it has to twist itself into a pretzel in order to please everyone to get the extra adulation and attention. Or, at this stage, at eleven or twelve, use the easily available drugs and alcohol may be used to gain group approval.

Eventually, overdrive and overcompensation to make up for a lack of confidence, for inferior feelings because you weren't loved enough could turn you into a successful accomplisher. It could also turn you into a nervous wreck.

So if at this stage, you have been provided with adequate information about your growing, maturing bodies, your parents understand your jumping on and off their laps in six different emotional directions, and they can put up with some rather peculiar language and twitchy behavior without making you feel like a total dork — you will be ready, as ready as anybody ever gets, for the first stage of real adolescence.

# Beginning The Search

The main task of adolescence is giving up parents as love objects to find new love objects, giving up identity as the parents' child to find a personal identity.

That was a very easy sentence to write. But it is the hardest thing anybody ever has to do, psychically, and practically nobody ever entirely accomplishes it.

## Giving Up Parents

The task is the same whether somebody has had good parents or terrible parents. Children idealize good parents so that nobody else is ever good enough or kind enough or loving enough, and children create idealized images of bad parents or missing parents so that nobody else is ever good enough or kind enough or loving enough. In either case, the task is to get over looking for your parents in the new people you love so you can see them and love them as they are, for themselves. But remember, this business of family relationships, family history, family expectations, family events, everything from divorce and death to illness and money problems forms a backdrop to all the upfront teenage problems, peer pressure, friendships, sex and drug problems and other social challenges. Family, parents, can really support — they can also tangle you up!

But if the task of detaching yourself from good or bad parents is the same, the solutions in each case are different.

You are now twelve to fourteen. You are full of energy and drive (sexual, aggressive, and every other kind). You are able to think abstractly now about god and death and life and the future, not just whether to skateboard or shoot marbles tomorrow afternoon. This is scary enough. But you are also now full of the emotional turmoil that comes with trying to give up old loves and the old family before you've really got new ones to take their place. This gap between the old and the new produces loneliness. You begin to feel real loneliness, isolation, depression very intensely, perhaps for the first time.

This is the age, in cases of bad parenting for the beginning of juvenile delinquency, for boys especially. It is the result of unformed conscience and the search for something to love, to belong to, to fill the life, as escape from loneliness and depression. In very rural places or inner cities, homes where kids are latch-key kids, situations where young children are left early unsupervised, this phase can begin as young as seven or eight. For girls, although they too may resort to juvenile delinquency, there are other forms of destructive behavior. Self-mutilation. Eating disorders. Bad relationships. These are increasingly prevalent (the last figures were as high as 40%) as girls as young as eight and nine years old dream of fashion-model thinness and appearance.

*Jill was the oldest of four children, age thirteen. Her father was an alcoholic, and though she loved him, he was there-but-not-there emotionally, as alcoholics can be. Her mother had to take care of four young children and work part-time to make ends meet and was naturally too tired to give Jill adequate mothering. Her mother wasn't particularly warm to begin with, and Jill lacked the early cuddling she needed. Until Jill was about thirteen, she tried very hard to get her mother's approval and affection by helping to take care of her younger brothers and sisters, overcompensating (trying too hard) to get love. But her mother was too tired to love her, and her father drank, so Jill, driven by early adolescent needs, went elsewhere. With her father as an example of how to escape reality (and an inherited propensity for alcoholism/ addiction), Jill joined a group of girls who used and pushed hard drugs. The group was led by an older girl on whom Jill had a crush. The situation filled all Jill's needs. A new love object to satisfy her emotional needs, escape from loneliness, and a dulling of the constant anxiety of inner turmoil and having to face the bleak reality of her world.*

Jill's behavior is called acting out — as opposed to working out conflicts in your head or talking them out with someone else. Unhealthy people act out their conflicts again and again (repetition compulsion), recreate the same emotional situations over and over, without being able to learn from experience, without understanding why they repeat destructive behavior, without being able to put an end to it. As Erik Erikson says, the source of neurotic tension is conflict repressed, not outgrown. Without the help of counseling, Jill may go on looking for mothering and ways to fight off the depression the lack of mothering has caused. With help, she may learn to get over what is now a lost cause: she will never be able to recapture the parental love she didn't have to begin with. No one can make her childhood up to her. We don't seem to be able to forget the past, but if she can learn to shrug it off, live with it, learn to parent herself and even others, she will be released from old needs to find new loves and her own identity as a person separate from her family. She will enjoy her friends more, and pick better friends, when she does not need them for parent-substitutes. She will be able to move on.

More normally, instead of acting out, an early adolescent will use fantasy as an outlet —sex fantasies, love fantasies, adventure fantasies. This is a terrific age for lolling around dreaming of heroes or of the hideous fate of enemies. A lot of excess energy and emotion can be released in fantasy, and many early teens spend more and more time away from the family, shut up in their rooms. Fantasies help adolescents try out different roles and feelings, especially the ones they are afraid of in the real world.

### Homosexual Feelings

Two of the most disturbing feelings at this age are increased homosexual feelings for those who are gay and lesbian (with the fear of being found out and the stigmatism perpetrated by society's moralizers) and homosexual feelings even among heterosexual teens, with the same fears. The second disturbance— and this will be more intense in middle adolescence — is the anxiety of independence versus dependence on parents.

Homosexual feelings, while perfectly normal for gay and lesbian youth, may confuse heterosexual teens. These feelings reflect a need for an important and intense relationship with a friend of the same sex. The friend isn't just any old chum as it was in preadolescence. He or she represents what Peter Blos calls the "ego ideal" and "represents the missing perfections of the self." One searches in the other person for all the things one wishes for in oneself, both emotional and physical qualities.

**Friendships**

A girl I know in her early teens invariably picks as friends or has crushes on girls who are tall and thin, and have straight hair. As you may imagine, she is small, a little plump, and her hair frizzes at the suggestion of rain. There are other qualities she picks. Being frantic, she looks for serenity. Being chronically insecure, she looks for cool. Being a compulsive babbler, she thinks silence means superior wisdom. (Wrong. Some people are silent not because they are deep, but because they just have nothing to say.)

Many of these intense relationships are short-lived because nobody can live up to the fantasies we spin around them, and once they are seen as ordinary human beings the thing is over. Another aspect of fantasized relationships is that they stand for, in boys, what the idealized father is, and, in girls, the mother. During this period, a teenager uses a friend as a sort of directive, wanting to be like the friend. If heads are healthy, everybody trots off in the right direction, toward doing well in school, in sports, in community effort. If heads are not healthy, the idealized friend can lead others off to minor places of pain that include tattoos and piercings — or major places of pain, into self-mutilation, into drug scenes and sex scenes and crime scenes.

But teen friendships can serve important positive functions. Friendship helps people to transfer feelings about their parents toward other people. It helps people get over earlier narcissism, a self-love that underlies the notion the entire world revolves around you and no one else. A good relationship with a friend can help turn the eyes outward toward the world of others, turn eyes into windows instead of mirrors that only reflect one's selves.

## Experimenting with Independence

Parents find their children more difficult now. Sometimes children emotionally disappear, sometimes they are as needy as ever. Sometimes they work harder than ever at school, sometimes they can't cope. They may sometimes number among the missing for a couple of hours, even if they've always been reliable before about letting people know where they are.

What's happening is that the early adolescent is experimenting with independence, and what parents may not always realize is that this is giving their child as many anxiety attacks as it's giving them. Their child may not be ready to run off to sea yet (take a subway to Coney Island, join the Peace Corps, hitchhike to California, live on a kibbutz), but he or she has begun to adventure and dare to be missing in action — even if it's only sitting through a movie twice, being late for dinner, and the devil be damned.

Adolescence is not just puberty, not just changes in the body. Early adolescence requires dealing with and resolving earlier childhood conflicts and beginning to transfer feelings away from parents. In adolescence proper, about fourteen to eighteen, the major breakthrough happens. Or it doesn't.

# Section Four

## ADOLESCENCE

# Who Am I?

The scene is the family dinner table with Mother, Father, Jack, aged sixteen, his younger brother Martin, aged thirteen.

MOTHER: Isn't it wonderful, Bill, having two such perfect sons? (*Mother hands out a lot soothing goodies like that to create an atmosphere of love and happiness, which is okay except that she takes it as a personal affront if her love isn't enough to make everybody happy, despite the private misery of having, say, failed an important exam or not made the soccer team or not gotten a telephone call from a particular person. Mother hasn't figured out that growing and grown people often need understanding even more than they need affection. And need to feel real accomplishment more than her not-always-applicable praise.)*

FATHER: I'm pretty proud of them, too, Mary, but I wouldn't say they were exactly perfect. I mean, Jack's marks are good and he made the soccer team like I did, but he still hasn't decided what to do with his life. *(Bill has been the kind of father who substitutes directing and managing his family's affairs for affection and caring. When his directions aren't taken or his managing refused, he feels righteously that he has done all he can and withdraws his approval. Since his sons love him and are trying to identify with him, they are in constant conflict about how much of themselves to give up to earn his approval and how much of their own integrity to preserve to be able to approve of themselves. Bill has a strong need to prove his own life valid, to the extent of needing his sons to pattern their lives after his own. He doesn't understand that the teens are the time when teens need their parents to turn into consultants, not managers.)*

MOTHER: Jack is only sixteen, dear. He's got years to decide what he wants to do. *(Mary is trying to defend Jack, but she is more deferential to her husband than protective of her son. She knows perfectly well that Jack wants to be a photographer. She also knows perfectly well that this would infuriate Bill.)*

FATHER: I knew when I was twelve that I wanted to be a doctor.

MOTHER: Just look at Jack's hands, Bill. A surgeon's hands, just like yours.

FATHER: It's his mind I'm worried about—which could turn out to be like yours.

*(Mary smiles a hurt, brave smile. She had been a painter once, but since she had never either been very successful or earned a lot of money at it, Bill had emotionally blackmailed her into giving it up for something he considered wasn't a waste of time, running a little shop. She had been unhappy giving up her painting, but she had needed, because of her own childhood pro-*

*gramming, to please her husband. But having lost the battle for herself, she didn't know how to help her children win theirs. Besides, Mary was unconsciously projecting her own repressed creative needs onto her son Jack. Bill was money-and-success oriented, but he couldn't see his programming either. Neither Bill nor Mary understood risk. They wanted their children safe, not free, and if it chained their psyches to a post, so be it.)*

MOTHER: I'm sure Jack won't turn out like me, not with you for a father. *(Thinking—I hope he does, a little. All parents want to see something of themselves in their kids.)*

*During this parental exchange, all hell is breaking loose inside Jack. He is at the age when the whole set of teenage conflicts has hit him. He has to let go of his parents hands and cross over to stand with his own generation. He has to replace original passions with new passions. He needs his parents' protection and counsel sometimes, but he fears their discovery about his problems with his friends, his concerns over drugs and sex. And then not only is there the need for parental love and approval, especially by the parent of the same sex so he can fully identify himself, but there is an equal need to be himself.*

*The inability to give up gratifying one's parents prolongs adolescence forever. Do what they want and please them, thinks Jack, or do what I want? Lose them or lose myself? Fight back and risk my father's disapproval—don't fight back, and I won't be able to look at myself in the mirror for a week.*

*Jack sits silent for a few moments, struggling. Then a new jolt into Jack's psyche is thrown by baby brother.*

MARTIN: I haven't said anything about it before, because I've been thinking a lot. But now I just want to tell you that I've decided I'm going to be a surgeon myself. *(Martin's decision is partly an attempt to knock his brother out of first place. It is very annoying to be a younger sibling constantly in competition for affection, money, privileges, attention, and so forth. But his decision is partly something else. He has watched his older brother for years, banging his head against the wall in rebellion, fighting for the freedoms that came to Martin more easily because his brother had fought the battles before. Martin doesn't want to go through all that rage. Much better to have his father's approval secure, much more comfortable to do what is expected of him. Martin will never suffer as much as Jack will, but neither will he ever know the true joy of doing exactly what he wants to do.)*

*Jack can't be silent any longer. It's bad enough having his parents pass his life around the dinner table on a platter, but to have that little---- come off sounding like the Littlest Angel!*

JACK: *(Standing up, throwing down his napkin)* I don't have your mind or your hands. Or Aunt Jessica's eyes or grandfather's nose. *(He had once taken comfort in the safety of this kind of identification.)* I think I know what I want to be but I'm not sure I can do it yet. When I know, I'll let you know. And you can approve or not approve. But I've got to do it my own way. I've got to be what I need to be.

FATHER: *(angry)* Your own way, as you call it, will get you nothing but trouble and I'll be the one who has to pick up the pieces. And what is so precious about your way! Now sit down and finish your dinner.

JACK: Dinner! *(Jack storms out of the dining room)*

MOTHER: Don't worry, dear. He'll get over it. It's just adolescence.

Just adolescence! The worst crisis of life in most civilizations, and people are still saying, "just adolescence."

## Keep It or Leave It

The agony of breaking with the past so that new horizons are possible, so that you are not forever a hung-up child is an incredibly difficult feat. That outgrowing of the old, crippling orders that make no sense in your life (be a doctor, keep your linen closet clean, live on the farm because our family always has whether you like it or not, be athletic-it-makes-you-a-man, get married or what will people say, make money or what will people think and besides look how much your grandfather made) — these things have got to be shed. And since most of them are unconscious, it isn't easy. (You can figure out a lot of those directives yourself by being sensitive to how you feel when you're doing something you don't like. Am I cleaning up my room because I've learned I feel better being in a neat place? Or am I cleaning up my room compulsively because a voice in my head calls me a pig if I don't and I feel guilty? You can then decide whether to clean up your room or not on a rational basis with intelligence in charge, either to satisfy your own needs, or, grinning and bearing it, to please your mother's voice.)

Along with deciding what to shed, there is the problem of what to keep. An unhappy adolescent, an insecure one, often throws the baby out with the bath water, and in total rebellion will shed valuable directives and goals as well as undesirable baggage. Giving up old loves for new doesn't mean you stop loving your parents, but you love them with less need, less passion, less anger for the ways they couldn't help failing you. Anger and hate bind a child just as securely to parents as love does, and totally rejecting your parents' values to espouse their opposites simply means you are living a negative blueprint of your parents lives. You're still not free!

The whole business of life is to be free (which does not mean you do as you please about taxes and traffic lights and being on time for meals—cooperation and courtesy and contribution are part of freedom, partly because it feels good, partly because you save energy keeping people off your back). The point is psychological freedom. You can use your natural rebellion now to leave your original family to start out on your own, to have a whole psychological revolution— and really start again on your own. Use your outer rebellion to have an inner revolution—leave not only home, but all those agendas behind. See everything with new eyes, every day. Use intelligence, perception, insight to decide what's right—not tradition, not memory, not ten thousand years of the kinds of wrong decisions that still make wars that still kill children.

*(A good example to look at, discuss with your friends, is previous generations' decisions about division: the division into nations, for instance. Can there be division without war? From 30,000 feet up in an airplane, India isn't really yellow or the United States pink. There are no natural lines. If there were no lines between people, national, religional, would babies get killed?)*

During your middle teens especially, your confidence is shakey. Though you need love and approval, you also have to fight for independence and therefore risk rejection and pain, disappointment in yourself and the disappointment of your parents. It's time to make your own decisions, and some do it more tactfully than others. They are the ones with more assurance already built into them.

*Finding one's own identity is one major battle of adolescence. The other, based on reproductive instincts, is love-and-sex. During these years, often the two battles are intertwined.*

### Your Eyes: Windows or Mirrors?

In your search for what you are, nothing is nicer than to have a mirror of yourself in some else's eyes, a mirror that gives back a glowing report of how cool, groovy, and altogether terrific you are. Falling in love with someone who adores you and thinks you're absolutely perfect is really very soothing to the ego. Adults know (at least a few do, anyway) that true, lasting love is based on seeing the other person objectively, loving that person as she or he is, forgiving the differences.

In adolescence, the adored person is usually used to hang one's fantasies on, mother images, father images, hero images (rescue me from my loneliness, rescue me from my boredom, rescue me from my parents, rescue me from my own thoughts, my life, myself, just rescue me, rescue me, rescue me), and narcissistic images (tell me I'm right, perfect, marvelous). Teenagers often use each other in make-believe fantasy relationships—not seeing the truth, but making it up as they go along. And making it up beautifully. Teenage loves rarely have warts on the ends of their noses. But since adolescent love is not supposed to last forever, it can temporarily serve a great purpose. It gives you a great place to go when you feel bad. And loving someone else, especially romantically, helps you get over loving those primary love objects, your parents, a lot faster.

## Romance

There are some difficult problems with love at this stage. (At least they begin at this stage—for some people the problems go on and on.)

*One major problem is the word itself. In this country particularly, we use the word love to cover everything from ice cream to puppies, and particularly for an addictive, chemical dependency on another person exactly like an addiction to drugs or surfing or skateboarding. LOVE HAS NO OBJECT; IT IS A STATE OF BEING, NOT AN ADDICTION. What we call love is often simply possession (many parents really need to own their children, and lovers need to own each other), out of pride, to give a sense of security in a scary world, or because we are conditioned to behave in these ways. Where need comes in, love goes out.*

We'll use the word romance instead.

A big problem is that a lot of teenagers feel insecure about their ability to handle either the emotional or sexual part of romance. They feel they aren't ready, and yet they also feel some group pressure about the experience of sex. Because of earlier physical maturation, or abusive sex in the home, or because "everybody" else is doing it, or because of seeing sex on television, suggested in every ad, in every magazine, sex experimentation is beginning younger and younger. There can be only one thing to say about young sex. (No early adolescence is complete without an education in *safe sex*: to prevent pregnancy; AIDS; sexually transmitted diseases.) If you aren't ready, you aren't ready, and you probably have perfectly good psychological reasons for it. Don't let anybody push you into it. Some very sexually well-adjusted men and women did not begin their sex lives until their twenties. And besides, half the locker room and street and neighborhood boasting is just that—boasting. Almost nobody tells other people the truth about sex.

Another problem that sometimes plagues teenagers is the old saying that girls dream of "love" and boys dream of sex, and that girls are sometimes willing to trade sex for "love" and boys are sometimes willing to trade some degree of commitment for sex. Many people today believe that if it weren't for the difference in upbringing, boys and girls would have equal sex drives and equal emotional needs. Certainly, girls as well as boys want to touch and be touched, to have intimacy, to have orgasms. Adults forget to tell their young that there is magic in intimacy, that sexuality is a treasure. In learning about the plumbing, therefore, sometimes the joy is missing.

There are studies being done about girl babies and boy babies, and there are major differences biologically, biochemically, aside from the obvious. Boys are born with more musculature and a greater need to exercise those muscles aggressively. Girls are born with greater perceptual abilities. They understand their environment, people, emotions more quickly than boys, and as they grow up they use that understanding to get affection. This may lead to needing affection more than boys seem to, as boys use their prowess, first physical, then intellectual, to get appreciation for performance. Upbringing enhances this situation, so that boys think they're unworthy unless they perform, and girls think they're unworthy unless they are adored.

This could probably be evened out early by teaching girls to enjoy accomplishment and achievement instead of playing "adorable," and by teaching boys they are worthy as persons without always having to perform. But so far, there is still the problem of girls needing approval and "love" from others to feel good about themselves, and boys feeling they aren't men unless they are performing well, even sexually. The combination of this sometimes causes disadvantaged teenage girls to want babies for loving confirmation of their womanhood, and boys to prove their manhood by fathering as many babies as possible. It's still hard for a girl to openly enjoy sex. Girls are still taught sex is bad so they won't get pregnant and ruin themselves for the marriage market. It's still hard for a boy to enjoy just being loved; perform, perform, or you're unmanly. The sad part is, boys need emotional care as much as girls (only it's unmanly to admit it), and girls need to take pride in accomplishing their own thing

(only it's too male-aggressive to admit it once you hit the age when you're manhunting—it upsets the male ego.)

Jack has a girl. When he leaves the dining room, he isn't sure whether to slam into his room and cope with his feelings alone or to call his girl and dump some of it on her. Or what would be even better, make love to her if she would let him. He decides to call, using the extension in the upstairs hall.

KAREN:      You sound awful. What's the matter?

JACK:        Just another one of those what-are-you-go-ing-to-do-with-your-life numbers and why don't you be a surgeon like daddy. And the repeat of I knew what I was doing at your age and watch out you'll be a bum, or at least a misfit like your mother.

KAREN:      Want to come over and talk about it? (*Part of her thinks, good, he needs me, loves me, I can care about his troubles, and he will love me even more. The other part of her thinks, why can't he handle his life as well as my daddy does, her ideal hero type. At Karen's age, only a small part of her thinks: this is a human being with needs of his own and problems to work out. She still mostly thinks of him in terms of her own images and needs.*)

JACK: Yeah, I guess so. (*Karen gets so analytical, Jack thinks. He knows that verbalizing love is a good feeling, but what he needs right now is physical love, and not the kind that stops short and drives you crazy. Jack blurts it out, his own need overriding Karen's.*) Karen, I love you, you know how much I love you. But I don't want to talk, I want to make love to you. If you're ready for love, why aren't you ready for sex?

KAREN: (*small silence, they've been through this often before*) If what you've got on your mind is sex, you aren't ready for love.

JACK: You know I am, you know I love you. It's just — oh, let it go. I'll be over in a few minutes. (*Jack, like everybody, has unconsciously picked what he perceives as the image of his mother in his first girlfriend. Karen is warm, creative, comforting, on his side — and withholds in the crunch, not only sex, but physical affection. Now, this is reassuring to Jack in many ways. Later, he must learn to pick a girl or woman who suits his adult needs rather than the remembered mother of his childhood. Some people pick a positive image of a parent — some people pick a negative image, a person exactly*

*the opposite of a parent. Either way, immature*
*people base love objects on their parents.)*

Karen, of course, is left sitting there with the usual problem. Shall I keep on refusing and maybe lose Jack's love? Or shall I give in and hate myself? Or do I really want to make love as much as he does only I'm afraid of getting pregnant and/or the wrath of my mother, father, and/or god? And will Jack think worse of me if I do, am I just being used, will he tell anyone and ruin my reputation so I get called a slut in school — and on and on and on. If loving is hard for a boy (surrendering emotions feels unmasculine to an immature male psyche), the question of sex, pill or no pill, even condoms for safe sex, is still hard for a girl.

It is, after all, her body that might carry the result of sex, the baby. And society still says "boys will be boys," but girls are bad girls if they have sex.

Girls are driven earlier into romantic feelings about boys because, while boys are praised for collecting achievements, girls are praised for collecting a boy. But there are other reasons for too-early attachments.

- There is a big shift now in what psychologists call cognitive processes: your brain is learning to think abstractly, not just concretely. What this means is that your brain can also drive you crazy now. Before, thinking and action were the same. Now thinking is imaginative. You can sit for hours listening to music and remembering, painfully, what a dork you were at school, and imagining it is all anyone is talking about. When you're sitting by yourself imagining the worst, a girl-friend or boyfriend is reassuring.

- The social world isn't the same. You used to play with anybody. Now, there is the beginning of race, ethnic, economic, gender orientation distinctions. For some teenagers, the social world, who you eat lunch with, what events and parties you go to, what crowd you hang out with, what behaviors and clothes are cool — all this is the means of gaining prestige. For others, the social world is a painful business of not fitting in, or of the constant conflict between fitting into the group and what you are yourself as a person. Here, too, to have a personal person of your own is something to fall back on.

- Friendships can be difficult. This is the first period in your life when real friendship is possible, concern for someone else, an ability to accept another person's flaws, to learn the skills of friendship, support, open-ness, trust, responsibility, honesty, an ability to resolve conflicts, to listen to the other person's views. But these are difficult skills, sometimes teenagers fail the first attempts at friendship. Again, it is easy to fall back on a boyfriend or girlfriend you "own."

- Family and life events can be traumatic, because everything is felt so intensely with your new cognitive, imaginative, abstract-thinking skills. Divorce, death, disease, disabilities — you feel deeply about these events and problems now, and a mate helps you get through them with physical and emotional affection.

- Who am I? But the most consuming crisis of all during the teenage years is still the separation from your original family and the discovery of your own personal identity. What kind of person am I? Not just what profession, work, or career shall I have, shall I marry sooner or later, the opposite sex or my own sex, interracially, or my family's ethnic background, BUT *even more deeply, what is the meaning of my life, why am I here, where am I going, why was I born, why am I living, what in the world is the world about, what is god, why is there cruelty, what can I do about it, shall I live life for myself or for everybody's sake, and, even, stop-the-merry-go-round-I-want-to-get-off!*

Being in love is an excellent hide-out from all these problems. It feels worth it to hide inside of a relationship even for a few hours a day to escape from solving the big problems that face you for the first time: how to cope with your own brain, your life, your parents, god, the universe, and what you are doing on this planet to begin with. It's exhausting facing inner crises from morning till night about school, your social life, your future, sometimes just staying alive and unmolested in a hallway.

But sex is another matter, and for girls particularly. The best decision a girl can make about sex — and it sounds easy but it's not — is the one she can most comfortably (psychically) live with. Karen's problem is complicated by her knowledge that Jack often uses sex as a problem-solver and an antidote to his own depression rather than an expression of his love for her. And she knows what a short-term antidote sex is and that it doesn't solve Jack's problems.

It is interesting to note that, like many girls, Karen has chosen a "misunderstood" boy to love. Karen has learned, from her mother, that the way never to be abandoned is to be needed, desperately, as a child needs. If Jack had it all together he wouldn't need and therefore might leave her. If she can handle her own need to be needed, it will help free her from dependent relationships.

Peter Blos says there are two important dangers in the romantic-sex part of adolescence in today's Western world model (Western dating habits are beginning to spread all over the world, even to China and India where marriages have traditionally been arranged between suitable families). One is the rush into locked-in relationships before a separate, defined personality has formed — losing your own identity in someone else's personality instead of finding out what you are first. The second danger, he says, lies in the opposite direction — repressing all sexual impulses, which can lead to an inability to eventually partner someone at all. This is especially dangerous for girls, who are still expected to repress their sexuality, where boys more often are not. Ellen Rosenberg's 1995 book *Growing Up Feeling Good*, has excellent chapters about the physical maturing of teenage bodies; boyfriends, girlfriends, going out; peer pressure sex choices; safe sex and pregnancy responsibilities; sexually transmitted diseases and AIDS; drugs, drinking, and sex; parents and your decisions about sex; disabilities and sex; and good, general chapters about death, divorce, racial, religious, economic differences, and the impact of all of this on teens and their relationships.

## The Three Tasks of Adolescence

1. Finding out about yourself, all the selves, all the pieces, the conditioning, of your parents, society, the voices in your head, your psychological processes, conscious and unconscious — and understanding the whole point of learning is to be as free of the "me" —which is really just stuff you've been told or you've inherited— as possible. This way you can live your own life. You don't need an adult, parent or therapist, for this process. Talk to yourself. Listen to yourself. Watch yourself in your relationships and other people will mirror you to yourself. Read the book of yourself — and you'll understand the basics of all humanity. You may wear these jeans and I may wear those and in Tasmania they may not wear jeans at all. But underneath the clothes, we're all predators trying to kill each other, and we're all lonely, trying to connect.

2. Learning to love givingly, as an adult, instead of as a child who is always needy; learning to love people as they are instead of only in the way you need them to be.

3. Facing the real world. Gathering the courage to cope with it independently and without too many emotional hang-ups from childhood getting in your way.

*Be cheered, if you're thinking you'll never make it home free. Almost nobody does. Jesus did, and Buddha, and Lao-Tsu, and Krishnamurti, and many women who were either not allowed to speak in public or if they did got burned at the stake as witches. They got free of their self-centered selves and to the other side of suffering, most of them in their teens. I personally had to suffer for a long time. Most do. And you?*

# Coping With Yourself

Larry, fifteen, bites his nails, fiddles with his hair, rubs
and scratches all over, taps his feet, drums his fingers,
talks in bursts of intensity, eats a lot, races around doing
anything and nothing, builds and collects things, works on
one hobby or project after another or several simultaneously,
anything from skateboarding to computer surfing to cars.
He works hard and well at whatever he does, including
schoolwork. Even in conversation, he pursues a point so fer-

*vently he often drives it into the ground. He does a lot of horsing around, plays practical jokes, pushes, nudges, pokes members of his family and friends.*

*This frantic activity alternates with boredom (a form of angry depression when you've exhausted your own inner resources and there's no input from the outside world of people or activities ) — and at Larry's age it's a special kind of boredom. It includes not only the mind (what shall I do with myself, I don't feel like doing anything), but also the physical sensation of I-can't-move-a-muscle-even-if-somebody-could-come-up-with-a-suggestion. During his periods of boredom Larry does idiot stuff just to keep busy, like Online games, taping MTV rock videos, cutting and dying his hair green, spending hours on the telephone with his girlfriend, piercing and tattooing yet one more piece of under-mutilated flesh, and cutting Coke cans in half and smashing them together. His mother finds a couple of dozen of these in his closet, he's collecting them, and thinks her bright, energetic Larry has gone mad. He hasn't. He's coping very well.*

### Can Parents Help?

His mother knows she could help him cope even better, but she also knows that a lot of the time now, Larry gets angry at advice. He may have seen his parents as his rock of emotional Gibralter in childhood, an activity-organizer, homework-helper, chore-supervisor, friendly dispenser of overnights, allowance, sports uniforms, and general support system in grade school. Now he sees them as intrusive, controlling, ignorant of all he has to face on a daily basis, of his problems. He sees them as unsupportive, nagging, full of unrealistic expectations, obsessive interest in his private life, judgmental, jealous. And Larry's reaction to her questions and offer of helpful advice is downright unfriendly. He's gotten over the newness, the move from middle school to high school. But at fifteen, he's beginning the journey to adulthood, struggling to define himself, make his own choices. It is a time when he may need help making decisions, a time when he may want to take control of his own reins — is even excited at the notion — and yet is unnerved about taking charge as well. He faces some important choices about what to do about his urgent sexuality, what to do about the party scene, how serious he is about school academically, whether he wants to go to college and if so, where, and if so, can he keep his marks up, and if so, what kind of future work does he want training for. A lot of this also involves his choice of friends now, and who he wants to hang out with.

Larry knows he could use some advice. But it also makes him angry because accepting help makes him feel like a helpless child again when what he is most trying to do is become an independent adult. Another problem his mother has now is reaching her once-open son on any emotional level. And she has a bigger problem: all the skills she had mothering him in infancy and childhood won't help her now as a teenager's mother: she has to develop new sensitivities, new understandings of changing daily problems, new ways both to set limits and permit freedoms, guide and suggest without too much controlling, and above all, to see that being a parent is not the same thing as a popularity contest.

## Can Defenses Help?

Larry defends himself against the threat of being overpowered by family emotions, loves, angers, disappointments, and by family expectations which threaten his own still-fragile sense of identity — by intellectualizing. He turns most discussions into solid facts and figures he can rely on instead of the unstable area of feelings. He fights as many feelings as possible with logic, his own kind of logic. His younger sister has been invited out on her first date and is very excited and happy. Larry says to his mother, "But the kid trips over his feet just walking down the hall, so how can she go out with him?" Larry is intellectualizing the disturbing feeling that his sister might substitute a new hero for her older brother. He teases his sister unmercifully. Humor is a terrific defense mechanism against emotion — some people can joke the love, hate, pain, anger away until they feel nothing.

Another emotion Larry is coping with here is envy. Larry has dated, had a girlfriend he really cared for, but he displaced too many emotional needs from his mother to the girl, and she got scared off. He has a new girlfriend now, but he's scared to trust his feelings to someone else.

**Can Drugs and Alcohol Help?**

He's also afraid of how available drugs and alcohol are at school and at the clubs he and his friends go to. Last week, at a rave in a garage outside of town, he saw kids as young as eight doing pot and crack cocaine. He and his friends were offered ketamine (Larry knows this wrecks the mind) and FX, the colorful fluid that can cause long-term brain damage. There were club drugs, designer drugs, white powder diluted into drinks too easy to overdose on. He's seen kids stop breathing and collapse into coma. He's seen friends of his who are girls get raped because no one was in control. LSD and inhalants were everywhere, a lot of his friends' parents made alcohol and pills easy to get. They had a survey at school. A lot of the parents were baby boomers who talked about their own drug use openly and shrugged it off when told that drug use among 12-to-17-year-olds more than doubled from 1992 to 1996. Half of everybody in these grades did at least pot and alcohol, and the parents said they had too little influence to stop them.

**Is There Somewhere to Go Besides Crazy?**

Larry's mother was not all that cool when she was young. Like other veterans of the sixties, she quotes:

*When I took drugs I saw God!*
*What did God say to you?*
*Don't take drugs.*

and does not understand that the problem Larry faces is less that he needs or wants to get high, but having his friends like him, approve of him, accept him. He can't explain to her that his major problems right now do not always involve his future: they involve whether or not to be part of the drug scene; and that, as sexual as he feels, he hasn't got the slightest idea how to make love to a girl.

All of this nowhere-to-go-but-crazy makes Larry lonely off and on. He's trying to cut away from family emotional ties, but so far there isn't much to take their places. He feels isolated and at loose ends. Because it's hard for him to be really close to anyone right now, it makes him feel as if no one really understands him, understands his needs and the values he is forming. It makes him touchy, argumentative, explosive sometimes. There is a growing rage in Larry because his parents don't always find his behavior acceptable, especially at times when feelings of inferiority plague him and he isn't even acceptable to himself. And in that isolation, because it's hard for him to compare emotional notes with other people, comes the loneliest sensation of all. "Nobody feels the way I do. I am alone." Mostly, Larry is active and pretty cheerful, but when the bad feelings come, they hit hard.

**Ages and Stages**

From about fourteen to eighteen, the psychic situation can feel desperate (unless you repress everything, in which case you simply have your adolescence later on, in your twenties or thirties or forties.) But sooner or later, you and everybody else has to go through the process of growing away from the family, of growing up. Think about Larry. It isn't easy. Think about yourself. It may be even worse.

Larry is driven wild by his basic drives: sex, anger (all kinds, mostly at authority and mostly at parental authority because he needs his parents and hates needing them), rage at his own failures and lack of enough world-experience, and very important, his drive to grow and mature into his own life. His conscience does a lot of guilt trips (you should be on time for practice, you shouldn't think about sex so much, you should be a better son, student, worker, friend, and on and on). Some of this is good. A little self-clubbing makes you try harder in life to do well, and the results are often rewarding. Too much self-beating is obviously self-defeating — nothing you do will be worthwhile. Some inferiority feelings spur you on to do better, others ride your poor self to death on a fast horse.

But between Larry's basic drives and his conscience comes intelligent observation about what's right and needful to do and what isn't right and needful to do. And his brain also uses the confidence given him by a well-supported childhood.

**Defenses and Escapes from It All**

Larry also uses practically every defense mechanism he can lay his psyche on. He displaces much of his sexual drive with nail-biting, computer games, music, horsing around, collections, projects, and hard work. He even won the argument about getting his junior license to drive as soon as possible. He displaces other parts of his sexual drive and his anger and the need to grow, through intellectualizing, explaining life logically so his feelings don't show. There are, unfortunately, people who hide their deepest feelings and drives forever behind their intellects so that they can never get out and nobody else can ever get in. But at Larry's age, with so few adult outlets — a full sex life, a satisfying job, money of his own to spend, freedom to function as he pleases — intellectualizing is a way of dealing with so many intense needs.

Larry also uses humor as a defense. When it isn't used as a total blocking system for all emotion or in harmful humor at others' expense, laughter is a good way to turn bad stuff around until it's funny.

Larry uses forms of displacement like transferring his feelings onto other people. If he's angry at himself, or a friend, he'll explode at his father. If he's angry at his father, he'll displace it onto his mother or sister. Direct anger (or any emotion) is hard for Larry. He also represses this and other too-troublesome emotions or denies them outright or projects onto other people (you're angry, not me).

Group behavior is another defense mechanism against all those voices both inside your head and outside it. Larry does what is especially typical in the United States — he charts a lot of his behavior according to the rules of his group. Instead of reaching down inside himself as he will when he gets older for his own rules, he and his friends create certain patterns of behavior that they all share. It makes them feel more secure, and it also lessens the anxiety that standing out alone on a limb would bring. This way, he doesn't have to struggle over each action, each decision. He uses group behavior as a model for his own.

### The Whole Country Escapes from It All

The big displacements in this country for our basic drives seem to be food, television, sex, drugs, alcohol. Larry does a lot of computer and TV time, some drugs and alcohol, only sometimes food. His sister uses food much more often. Without the comfort of having a mate, she regresses to the familiar childhood comfort of food. The trouble is society's new revenge, what Naomi Wolf calls, in her book *The Beauty Myth*, *the Iron Maiden*: to be acceptable you have to be so thin you only eat when you're ready to faint. His sister is already agonizing over diets, dreams of plastic surgery, faces eating disorder problems. Like Larry, she has had a solid childhood. She may well find something more interesting to spend her life on.

### Other Problems

There are some problems Larry doesn't have, although he has friends facing all of them.

There are two friends on his soccer team who are black. When they were all younger, none of their school's families paid much attention. Now race has become an issue as they face adulthood: intermarriage possibilities can inhibit the kids from running in and out of each other's homes sometimes. Ethnic jokes, who feels superior to whom (I went to the same school as Haille Selassi's grandson, and he was forbidden to date me because his father was an Emperor: Ethiopian royalty did not date white girls). Religion has become an issue. Everyone used to play with everyone, and now suddenly people are supposed to stick with their own kind. Larry knows this kind of thinking is dangerous. Families, religions, races that stick together for security, lose that security. It isn't practical. If you include some people in, you leave others out. Like any gang or country or mob, any economic or social class, any caste or tribe, this invites attack from the ones you leave out.

Speaking of feeling left out, Larry's team's captain is gay. Mike is not effeminate, he does not molest little boys, he's not given to wearing girl's dresses, though all those things have been part of the normal fabric of civilizations everywhere in the world for thousands of years. But Larry's friend Mike has known for a long time he simply finds men attractive and would like to have a loving relationship with a boy his own age and not have to worry about being stigmatized. He doesn't want to date girls to cover up being gay like other gays sometimes do. He knew about himself early, although many teenage gays don't. He knows that 10% of the population is gay, meaning that a lot of parents have gay children. This kind of percentage of the population indicates that homosexuality is just another human trait.

Mike put it this way, explaining it to his friends. If one hundred kids are graduating in a class, ten of them are homosexual and twenty parents have produced them. That's too high a number to consider homosexuality at all abnormal. In addition, there is a high percentage of people who go through homosexual periods during their lives, or spend their lives as bisexuals, able to love members of both sexes. "If we sometimes act less than groovy," said Mike, "or seem nuts, it's because being persecuted or looked at as if you're less than a man if you're gay or less than a woman if you're a lesbian makes you insecure all the time. You can't see all those gay-bashing stories on television or read about lesbians being refused adoption papers for a baby, without feeling left out of the human race. At least if you're African-American or American-Indian (unless you're also gay or lesbian), you're got people just like you in your family. We have no one. There's no we're-all-in-this-together feeling, and home is the first place we're kicked out of."

It isn't easy to be a homosexual, as it isn't easy to be a part of any other minority group, but it's no more abnormal that being black, Hispanic, Jewish, a Frenchman in Kansas City, or a writer. It's just there are fewer around.

Larry (who, in many of the ways I've described him, could be a girl just as well — with the exception that Larry will be valued for what he can do, and she will only be valued for who wants her) will need to depend less heavily on defense coping mechanisms as he gets older. He will need many of those emergency measures less often as he gains perception in self-awareness and the strength to cope on his own with his drives and his guilts.

A good relationship with a girlfriend will eventually help relieve some drives and anxieties. So will a growing objective sense of useful accomplishment. The explosions, the racing around, the boredom (depression), most of the anger, will calm down as Larry's almost total confusion about what he is and where he is going is replaced by an increasing ability to look at those questions and find his way.

If all goes well with Larry, and his drives don't drive him crazy, into crime or violence or even just general mayhem, and his intelligence silences old voices so he can hear himself think, he can stop asking "Who am I and how do I cope?" and say instead, "Here I am — this is me."

# This Is Me

I f you are lucky, you have survived Middle Adolescence, both your internal and external demons, and made it into Late Adolescence, about eighteen to twenty. This is when you begin to master the trauma (shocks) of your first eighteen years, a task that may last you the rest of your life. Some people do it better than others. What's been imprinted on your brain stays there, for most of us. You deal with it daily.

The nature of the self (all those chattering selves) is chaos; a good definition of hell is self-absorption, to be locked inside your self with those selves. It's more fun to leave the inside of your brain to argue with itself and go out into the sunlight. Step out of your personality. Just live your life.

Those with an ability to find work they like and do it with satisfaction, to give and receive love (for some women and many men, receiving affection is harder because they feel that accepting loving attention is accepting help and it makes them feel weak, passive, as if they've surrendered themselves to childhood again), to understand the nature of themselves and their motives with humor and honesty — these are the people who can live life fully.

Nobody makes it through eighteen years conflict-free. Look at the members of your family. Look at your classmates, people in stores, on the streets, on television who are Chinese or African or from India, the Australian Outback. Give or take a few superficial differences like skin, hair, clothes, all human beings are alike in their brain functions: everybody's brain thinks. Thinking is the nature of the human brain, everybody's brain is noisy with chatter and conflicts. Not only are you not alone in what your brain does, there are 6 billion of us on the planet now: so loneliness is an attitude everybody's got, not a fact.

So. We're all in the same boat of conflicting drives, needs and greeds, a longing for security yet a desire for freedom, a spiritual yearning for connection to the universe instead of that terrifying sensation of being alone under the stars. Of course, as both Krishnamurti and Einstein said, we are all part of the universe and it is just a trick the mind plays telling us we are separate. But we're all in pain over this. **And we want to get out of our pain.**

## Dealing with Conflict and Pain

It's a good idea to look at some of the worst ways of dealing with the conflicts you may be stuck with forever, and some ways that are more helpful and constructive. What the brain, craving the security of order, does is organize a working personality so it can function (more or less) in this world. It either deals with or escapes its conflicts. Pain is natural, considering the nature of the human brain and the horror show it has made out of civilization. Pain will pass if you don't make it worse by dealing with it badly. If you deal with it badly, you've now got two pains — the original one, and a new one, the hangover from the way you dealt.

### ESCAPE

Instead of dissolving the conflict or psychological pain through insight into it, many people simply choose escape. Drugs, alcohol, gambling, sex, food, constant action, shopping, television — there are long lists of escapes used by human beings to numb pain. Occasional pleasure in these things is normal. Constant escape is one of the poorer ways of organizing your psyche or resolving conflict. For one thing, the problems are always still there when you come back.

## REPRESSION

*Barbara was brought up in a home where the word pleasure didn't exist. Her parents had such strong consciences themselves that no activity was permitted that didn't also serve a useful purpose, that wasn't in some way productive (gardening was okay because it produced vegetables the family could eat; reading was okay because it was good for the mind and schoolwork; bicycling was okay if you also did an errand). Her parents were close with money, close with treats, clothes, possessions that weren't useful. Even friendships were frowned on, partly because they wasted time, partly because outside influences might take Barbara's mind off productive goals (among other decisions her parents made for Barbara was that she was to be a "successful" lawyer). To reinforce her parents' values, the family went to church not once but three times every Sunday, and their religion reinforced the work-no-pleasure ethic very strongly. The materialism of the media was easily controlled: no television, no ordinary magazines displaying the culture's commercialism, as her parents called it, were permitted.*

*Although her parents never discussed sex, Barbara learned from her parents' reactions to her early childhood behavior and from the minister that there was something "bad" and "dirty" about it, and that she would lose both her parents' and the church's and therefore god's approval if she had anything to do with her own body or anyone else's. Barbara, dependent as a child, and particularly as a girl child, on the approval of her parents and of the church, could not bear the anxiety her sexual drives caused in her and repressed them from the onset of puberty. She also repressed her adolescent conflicts over her feelings about her parents. Consciously, Barbara did not experience her adolescence at all.*

Barbara turned out to be a very successful lawyer. She works from eight in the morning often till midnight, earning a good deal of money. She has no close friends. (She doesn't know how to be close to people; and if she tried, it might threaten her independence, suggest sexuality.) She has transferred her need for approval from her now-dead parents entirely to god and the church. She has few possessions, and the only pleasure besides work and the church her psyche allows her is art, which is okay because so much of the art she likes is religious.

Psychologists might say that Barbara has made the best of a bad situation. She copes with daily reality, functions in the world, sleeps fine at night. People who love her admire her, but they think it is sad that so much of Barbara is repressed. All work, so little love and pleasure.

Many people like Barbara don't make it at all. Barbara was brilliant enough to make it through, especially since she had been given a strong enough sense of self-worth. If she had been less bright, a failure, given to self-hate, she might have totally withdrawn not only from human relationships but work as well, and ended up a defeated human being, forbidden by parental law to reach another human for help, forbidden by her own mind to reach into her unconscious for the answers to her conflicts.

We all repress a lot of things in an attempt to keep our sanity and balance, especially from the early sexual feelings of our childhoods. It's often too painful to face. But Barbara's massive repression of her own sexuality could have been dangerous, and for a less gifted personality, would have been. You can quite literally repress yourself out of existence.

## REPETITION COMPULSION

*Jerry adored his father, who owned a small chain of shoe stores and managed them successfully. Jerry's father wanted Jerry to go into the business, and Jerry wanted it, too. When he graduated from high school, Jerry worked for his father for the summer. At first all went well. Jerry came in on time, did his work efficiently, often stayed late to learn more about the business from his father. His father was pleased. Then, after a few weeks, Jerry began to come in late fairly often, disappear at lunchtime, make excuses not to stay late. His mother, envious of Jerry's attachment to his father and hating his growing away from her, began making at first small demands (give mommy a few hugs before you go), and later larger demands on her son's time (pick up my dress at the cleaner during lunch break, darling, will you, I'm so tired today, and try to come home early from the store because I just can't cope with fixing the washing machine and you know your father never does anything for me and if I couldn't depend on you I don't know what I'd do).*

*Jerry is the middle of a tug of war.*

The tug of war goes back to when Jerry was four or five years old, when he was trying to identify with his father, but his mother wouldn't let him on the grounds that she loved and needed her son. The father wasn't around often enough to make sure mommy let go, in those days when men could comfortably ignore their children without actually getting a divorce and leaving town. And since it was nice for child-Jerry to think how much his mommy loved and needed him, he has become dependent on that kind of need. Unless Jerry thinks this through, he will spend his life setting up this situation for himself over and over again because it was never resolved in the first place. He will always depend on a woman's needing him too heavily and give in to those needs, so he'll never get to the office on time. He will use her as an excuse not to succeed at any job. He won't be able to say, "Not now, Agnes." And he will end by hating her as much as himself and blaming her for his failure to perform.

Repetition compulsion, the reliving of old patterns and conflicts, can be deadly unless people learn to see the reality of the situation. People who set up the same emotional situation again and again are unable to learn from experience; they just keep setting things up the same way. Girls may keep on falling in love with the wrong boys, or go on turning bosses into father figures. Boys may go on turning the anger they once felt against their mothers against girl after girl, or turn jobs into self-defeating situations because they hate authority figures.

Think about your own relationships with people. If you are a girl, do you look for girl friends who are very critical, maybe the way your mother was, and then get hurt over and over by their criticism? Do you look for boys who are punitive? Are you sure they love you like your father did and, like him, order you around out of so-called caring, and then get hurt because the boy isn't your father and really doesn't care about you at all? You repeat the earlier experiences to try to resolve them, get them over with once and for all. The trouble is you can never change the past. It's a lost cause. You have to figure out what went wrong and try not to repeat it again.

There are as many possibilities for repetition compulsion as there are qualities in people and people's relationships. You may have very small, not harmful, compulsions to repeat (like always combing your hair before dinner), or very large ones that block you from functioning (like repeating your whole childhood in every relationship to make it come out with the right ending at last).

## FIXATION

We've discussed fixations on parents and their rules, and we've discussed fixations at the various sucking, potty, and early sexual stages. But there are also fixations on defense or coping mechanisms of your personality that keep you from functioning freely. A fixation makes you unable to change, to adapt easily to new things, people, circumstances. It may cause you:

- To always displace your anger so you never confront the person you're really angry at head on. (This creates too much anxiety.)

- To always sublimate your emotions and sexuality so you never have to confront a real feeling about anything. (This creates too much anxiety.)

- To always regress to childlike behavior or tone of voice when the going gets rough rather than to face it with the responsibility of an adult. (This creates too much anxiety.)

- To escape every problem by disappearing into an addiction, not just drugs, or sex, but workaholism, shopaholism, body-building, body-starving, body-mutilation, television. (Facing anything creates too much anxiety.)

And so forth.

Late adolescence is the time when the force of reality takes over and channels your drives and your inner directives, copes with fixations and repressions, and tries to make the most out of all the things you are, good stuff and bad, and make one, whole integrated person. Take note. Mastering reality is something most of us never do completely, except now and then for brief, calm periods in adult life. Off and on, always, because we never seem to meet and resolve the challenges of life completely, everything that's ever happened to us comes back to plague us.

Oh, well. Nothing like a little pain to drive you on.

WORK

Late adolescence reorganizes a lot of the energy that was going every which way during your midteens into work. Along with the capacity to love instead of need, the ability to relate appropriately to others, your mate, your family and friends and community, to the stars, along with the capacity, that is, to relate rightly to yourself, other people, the air you breathe — is your growing capacity to relate properly to your work.

- The point is, to find work that suits your interests and talents if you can. If you can, you are among the fortunate. Many people need to break their backs in mines, on farms, in factories, begging in the streets.

- The point is, once you find work you like to do, be sure you do the work for its own sake, not for the sake of the acquisition of power, of greed, of status and position and ambition. These contaminate, and produce a world of ruthlessness, oppression, ultimately war.

- The point is, be sure what you do harms no one.

M any people discover, when their brains are trying to kill them, that work is an excellent distraction. Everything else can seem crazy and unreal — your boyfriend cops out on you, your parents drive you over the edge, the television news makes you hysterical with the state of the world, the future looks blank or worse, and your past is unthinkable — diving into an objective task that the objective parts of your brain can deal with is a terrific way of making order and sense out of something. Work can bind you to actuality when all else is chaos. It can satisfy all parts of the psyche at once. Work can use up a lot of the energy from your basic instincts, it satisfies your conscience that you are being "good" and "productive" and "useful," and it satisfies your personal agenda that you are mastering reality situations and joining the march of civilization. Many minority teens, who cannot get jobs because of racism or lack of transportation to get to a decent job suffer without these feelings, not to mention the lack of opportunity to learn job skills. If you are as intelligent as you are smart, your brain and body will be happy in satisfying the need of all life to grow and be all it can be, fulfill its nature.

The kind of work you do will vary, of course, from college studies to trade school to secretarial duties to climbing telephone poles. But the point is the same. It is an outward-directed activity that links you with what the rest of the human race is doing — and for it, you get rewards, good grades, money, pats on the back, the feeling of belonging in the world — in short, approval, your own and other people's.

The kind of work you choose can tell you a great deal about yourself besides that you have an interest. It can tell you about how you did not resolve the earlier conflicts in your life.

A psychologist may be someone who did not feel loved and understood as a child and turned that unmet need around to love and understand everybody else.

Sometimes those needs get twisted; and a lonely, frightened child can grow up to be a bullying nurse or a guard who mistreats prisoners.

Actors are often fixated at the self-love stage of childhood and need constant applause to feed unstable personalities and the emptiness that should have been filled by parental love.

People who had to try too hard for parental approval and who still need approval, often develop a great deal of charm. Many of these make good salespeople. The instant reward of a sale brings both money and approval.

The problem of the artist's personality is too difficult to go into, and besides nobody understands it very well yet. Obviously, there are some fixations: at the sucking stage (the artist needs more love than any mother could give and grows up needing it from the whole world); at the potty stage (the need to produce gifts from itself, the need to be tidy and organize things and thoughts in an orderly and acceptable way); quite considerable anxieties left over from early childhood sexuality. Obviously a lot of things are at work, including talent (we don't know yet what makes for gifted people), a need for encouragement and approval, the sense of being different, the personality that is still openly child as well as adult. And finally the fact that for artists, the only way to cope with anxiety is to write or paint or make music or perform. People who enjoy the arts are those who are aware of their need to connect with beauty, whether that is the spiritual beauty of a statue or book, the peaceful sacredness of a lovely church or temple, a fine painting, or the beat of rhythm and blues.

This description of artists includes all of us, at least in part. We all have talents of some kind, we all have pain that feels better when we work, conscious and unconscious. But in a world frantic to produce, possess, and consume, it is well to take care to enjoy work, not be driven by it. In a psyche frantic for approval and the material and psychological rewards it brings, it is well to be aware of contaminating your joy in work by competition and ambition.

It's rough pulling yourself together. It's hard to learn to love and work in satisfying ways that take your own needs and the objective reality of other people and the world into account. Sometimes, a lot of times, you can't. Some people fail altogether. Some people put off getting over adolescence and prolong the process of self-imprisonment into their twenties —or thirties, forties, or sixties. Some people accomplish part of the process and develop a few defeating behavior patterns created by their own terrors along the way.

But if you can manage to get through adolescence without losing your mind, take heart. The developmental states of the human psyche are about to stop, temporarily, creating tidal waves. There is a short period of moderate calm ahead. Young adulthood. After that, it's one crisis after another again.

P.S.   There is a point to all this hard work. If you're thinking — "I don't matter. What I do doesn't matter" — think again. Everything in the universe is connected to and affects everything else. Therefore, *everything matters*. From physics to psychology, the behavior of matter, including human beings (we are, after all, all made of the same molecules, the same stardust as everything else), makes waves. Just breathing in and out affects the atmosphere — and the universe doesn't need any more bad breath!

*Section Five*

# ADULTHOOD

# Nothing Stays The Same

Adults and adulthood can be confusing to young people. You take a look at your parents one year and they're the same as last year. You take another look next year, and they've changed. Which is annoying, because you're having enough trouble already, without the scenery shifting around you. Your mother should stay the way your mother is supposed to be and your father the same, and also your siblings (like them or not), because personality change is something you have to cope with, and it's annoying to cope with someone else when you have all that work to do coping with yourself.

Yet nothing stays the same, because one of our basic drives as human beings is to grow, to fulfill our natures. It's the old bit about whatever stops growing, dies.

It's as true for adults as for young people. There are passages at every age for people to struggle through — if you're interested in what happens to adults in their mid-life crises, which usually happen about the time you hit your teens — read Gail Sheehy's *Passages*.

Anyway, your scenery remains the same for a while and then:

Your mother hits her mid-thirties, spends a couple of months banging at her computer with one hand, tearing her hair out with the other, screams at you like a cockatoo to clean up after yourself (after the fifteen years or so you've gotten used to "maid service"), and it's a definite shock to your system. She further announces she's sick of grubbing around the house and is going back to designing jewelry, which is where she started out before she got interrupted by babies (an assault on your ego and sense of your own importance). And then you find yourself not only getting your own dinner occasionally, cleaning up (or not) your own room, and even having to pitch in on her work like taking out your garbage, but she is not nearly as available to discuss your problems, bolster your ego, feed your face, adore, worship, and venerate at your shrine as she was before. It's appalling. But wait till you hit your own mid-thirties and feel trapped in conditioned roles and places in your life that just aren't enough to nourish your soul.

Your father hits forty. The morning of his birthday he wakes up looking gray, a little pinched around the mouth, and, if you peer closely, the faintest traces of madness lurk in his eyes. Don't panic. It's going to get worse, not better. You will catch him staring at your mother as if he'd never seen her before (has he got the right wife?), glaring at you (how did you get big enough to make him forty, and who in blazes are you anyway with your big feet and your noisy friends and where did the twenty dollars he gave you last week go?), and more and more often you will hear him complaining about or watch him quietly worrying about his job. This is the age at which men and women go through an identity crisis very much like the crisis of adolescence. Who am I? What does it all add up to? I'm halfway through my life and where am I? Am I married to the right person? Does my job fulfill my need for growth? Are my children going to be all right and have I done right by them? What happened to the dreams of my youth and what lies before me? And, for the first time, what will happen to me when I get old, if I get sick, if there isn't enough money for the children's college or other needs? And also, for the first time, death looms as a real possibility not just as someone else's nightmare. Fortyish is really hard on the nerves. Go easy if you can.

And it can be hard your nerves, too, the scenery changing.

Divorces, job changes that mean moving someplace new, parents preoccupied with their own change and growth (necessary because if they aren't living fully and rightly, they can't help taking some of the bitterness out on you, and they certainly can't teach you what they don't know about living) — all this change is difficult to cope with, and it all affects you.

People grow and change at different rates as they get older. And some people stop growing entirely. Those who can accept and enjoy changing patterns in one another, and who can forgive each other's differences, find it easier to hang in there together than those who can't. But sometimes even those who can accept change grow in such different directions (or one of them grows and the other stays in a rut) that the relationship becomes impossible. All of it will affect you as a young person, and eventually you'll go through it yourself.

Somebody once said that it is ironic that the two most important decisions people have to make in life, their choice of work and their choice of a mate, have to be made when they are too young to have any experience to go on. True. But it's also true that maybe only young adults have enough energy to be able to make such decisions. It's harder to find courage to make and remake and unmake decisions later on.

Happily, after late adolescence, for most people things settle down a bit. You may experiment for a while with different relationships, different pursuits (jobs, education, travel, goofing off for a while), but you will eventually pick someone to mate with and something to do. You will form goals in terms of permanent relationships, accomplishments, life style. These efforts will absorb a lot of inner conflicts, and the emphasis will now be on proving you're worth something, proving your independence. Unless you've gotten locked into the "rescue" fantasy — mom (or a mom-substitute like a wife/husband will save me, take care of me, or the fates will or I'll get lucky, so that instead of mastering tasks to make it on your own, life in general is somehow supposed to come to the rescue in the form of a person or an overnight miracle.)

If work strengthens the confidence, marriage (with or without the piece of paper, opposite or same sex), and parenthood are still necessary for psychological maturity for most people — the commitment to adult roles, relationships, responsibilities. Being an adult, identifying with adult behavior (meaning, I can-take-care-of-myself-now-and-others-if-need-be), frees you at last from being your parents' child; and with this resolution of childhood dependencies, you can now identify with instead of fight your parents, and your emotional life should be far more orderly for a while.

Aside from the growing capacity to work, the growing capacity to love is what shapes adulthood. As a child you needed to receive warmth and love much more than you were able to give it. In your teens, physical and emotional desperation and a need to recreate or replace parent images prevented you from seeing other people clearly enough to truly understand their needs. In the kind of adult love that lasts and nourishes through whatever comes along, the trick is not only to be able to give as well as receive affection, but love freely and not destroy someone else with your own needs, the needs that did not get met from your parents when you were a child. Parent images can be hang-ups forever if you let them. Adult love is a state of freedom: it is not possessive, jealous, or a certificate to own or colonize another human being.

The ability to love and to work are shaped by your past conditioning and prejudices, until you see these and let them go. The fewer chains you drag from childhood into your twenties the better. In your twenties, either because nature insists on an emotionally quiet period so you have time to mate, nest, start to earn a living, or because you decide the world out there is more interesting than you are yourself, you'll experience a period of apparent mental health. Toward the end of your twenties, whatever personality problems (and we all have a few) you've managed to accumulate will become clearer to the eye. If the chains aren't too heavy, you can probably drag them through life. If they're tripping you up, yell for help. It's idiotic not to set a broken psychic bone the same way it's idiotic not to set a broken leg. We're always coping with our pasts in our present. But it shouldn't be such an overwhelming struggle that we go down, beaten to death by our own ghosts.

Erik Erikson describes the Eight Ages of Humans as follows:

1. *Basic Trust vs. Basic Mistrust.* The first stage, when babies learn to trust the world or not, depending on the care they get. If it's good, their egos grow strong and sure, their personalities warm and giving, they have a feeling of belongingness. In the absence of care, depression and withdrawal from reality can take place.

2. *Autonomy vs. Shame and Doubt.* The toilet training stage if it's handled well produces people who have a sense of control without loss of self-esteem, goodwill and pride — it makes for givers. Overtraining creates manipulators, power-hungry types, miserliness, shame (rage turned against the self), sadists, takers. Overtrained children are forever terrified of losing control and remain self-doubters.

3. *Initiative vs. Guilt.* The early sexuality stage. Everyone needs to try, to experiment, to discover for oneself. The urge is strong at this age, but if a child is too overwhelmed by being made to feel too guilty over discovering its own body as well as loving the parent of the opposite sex too much, all initiative may be dampened.

4. *Industry vs. Inferiority.* The latency period. The first real attempt to make it outside the womb of the family, in

school, on the baseball field, in the orchestra. The danger here is [COMPARISON—my own word in caps] failure, and long-time feelings of inferiority.

5. *Identity vs. Role Confusion.* Adolescence. The need to establish one's own identity, within oneself, in the eyes of someone loved, in the group, in both sexual and occupation roles.

6. *Intimacy vs. Isolation.* Young adult. You know yourself and can cope with yourself and so love and nurture others — or you remain adolescent and just go on searching for your own identity through the mirror eyes of others. This in itself condemns you to loneliness.

7. *Generativity vs. Stagnation.* Adult work. Whatever you do should give you the feeling of being productive, of serving life, whether it's having a baby, fixing a car, making enough sales to satisfy yourself. If you don't feel productive, you'll end in boredom, depression, the sense of going nowhere. For some people, just a paycheck is enough to bring a feeling of a good week's work. For others, climbing Mt. Everest is a major necessity. Suit yourself.

8. *Integrity vs. Despair.* You've either lived in a way that satisfies your soul as you get older or you haven't. There is a need in all of us to have made a difference,

no matter how small or how dearly paid for. We seem to need to make a contribution, to serve, to give back what we have been given.

I like Maya Angelou's approach: she says, "What you learn, teach. What you have, share."

*Anyway, once you have made your way through all these understandings, you are an adult. Good luck.*

Only remember, in your search for yourself, that your self is the problem, not the holy grail. This is where modern therapy has gone wrong for the most part. The point is not to have a stronger self, but to dissolve it so it doesn't get in the way of your life.

In these brains of ours is crammed everything that has happened to us for millions of years (biological past, biochemical past), everything pertaining to our particular cultural past (gender, race, ethnic past), everything in our own personal past. A lot of baggage. Heavy. Dump some of it. Obviously, you need to remember how to speak a language. You need to remember your address. You need to remember how to do what you do to earn a living. But you do not need to remember to hate what you were taught to hate, or to set yourself apart. I mean, you can be a woman without doing woman all the time; you can be black without doing black; be WASP or Chinese without doing WASP or Chinese. It isn't necessary to carry psychological passports.

*Section Six*

---

# THEORIES OF HUMAN BEHAVIOR

# *And Then There Was Light*

**Mental Illness: Attitudes, Theories, Treatments**

B F. (Before Freud) or at least well into the 1700's, people with mental illness were in large trouble. The best fate an emotionally ill person could expect was to be kept unseen and unmentioned and untreated in the farther reaches of the household. More often, the psychiatrically ill terrified everybody and ended up being burned at the stake as witches or chained in dungeons and left to scream, rot, and die as fast as possible. Some communities prayed to them as shamans, priests, or spiritual healers, or exorcised them to drive out the evil spirits. But most people with severe mental illnesses were subjected to imprisonment in asylums such as the St. Mary of Bethlehem asylum in London. Known as Bedlam, the asylum was a pit of chaos. The administrators charged an admission fee to visitors wishing to view the patients' unusual behavior. The asylums of today are the large state-owned institutions.

The treatment of people with mental illness is improving. Research in neurobiology, psychology, sociology, and brain chemistry has resulted in a better understanding of the causes of mental illness. This has led to more effective and humane treatment.

We've been discussing some of the elements of psychology we know about: developmental psychology; racial-memory psychology; cultural-social psychology. We understand, as the philosopher/teacher Krishnamurti points out in his book *Education and the Significance of Life*, that while of course we need technical knowledge and memory for skills (no point in reinventing the wheel or brain surgery), psychological memory imprisons the individual and hinders the very freedom that is the whole point of education, of being alive.

With understanding, research, and treatment, we can help to free those with mental illness.

With self-knowledge, a willingness to let old structures decay, and start on new ground with new values, we can free ourselves from all the destruction we cause, to build a whole new world.

Light has been trying to get through all these walls of all the mental houses we build for ourselves because we want security instead of freedom. The joke, remember, is that there is no security. We might as well just step out into the light and be free.

There have been carriers of the torch along the way.

## A Brief History

The ancient Greek physicians were the first to recognize that mental disorders are caused by physical and emotional factors, and they were the first to include mental disorders in medical practice. Before then, people with mental illness were exorcized to cast out the infestation of evil spirits and were treated by religious ritual. Greek medical opinion on psychiatric illnesses was summarized by Hippocrates in the fourth century B.C. He felt that psychiatric illnesses were caused mainly by diseases of the body, and he wrote accurate descriptions of hysteria, depressions, and manic disorders.

The physicians of Rome adopted Greek medical principles and thought mental illnesses were caused by body "humors" or imbalances. It was very primitive psychiatry, but at least the psyche was treated within the realm of medical practice. After the fall of Rome, Greek and Roman medicine was largely forgotten, and people believed once again in the demon theory of mental illness.

By the sixteenth century, physicians once more took arms against the persecution of the mentally ill and advocated medical treatment. Johann Weyer published the first book in the West on psychiatric disorders. In the seventeenth and eighteenth centuries, more physicians studied and experimented with the problems, but still most patients were ignored or imprisoned either in ordinary jails or in hideous lunatic asylums like Bethlehem (shortened, our word 'bedlam,' meaning total uproar, confusion). By the nineteenth century, public and private psychiatric hospitals and wards of hospitals were being built. However, doctors still felt the causes for mental illness had to be physical disorders of the brain. (There are some rather gruesome stories of surgical procedures done on unwilling victims in quest of the brain's secrets.)

**Several Basic Approaches**

FREUD — THE INNER WORLD

It wasn't until the early years of the twentieth century, with the work of Sigmund Freud, that psychiatrists and psychologists came to understand the emotional, not merely physical, causes for mental illnesses. It was the great genius of Freud that first uncovered and explored the unconscious mind. He revolutionized medical thinking about mental illness, personality development, and the treatment of the emotionally ill, and founded psychoanalysis as a method of helping people gain understanding of, then resolving their psychological problems. Most development psychology today rests on the groundwork of Freud's insights into human behavior. His followers today, though they may differ from Freud in some ways, all agree on one major theory of human behavior: *personality is an outward expression of inner need*. A patient in treatment (therapy) therefore is to talk in a special kind of way, a process called free association — saying anything that comes into the mind rather than intellectually thinking out the conversation — in order for the therapist to understand what the person's needs and problems are and to help the patient meet these more successfully rather than find defeat at every turn.

The aim of psychotherapy is to uncover the conditioning, the trauma, the personal memories and experiences, the places where people are stuck and hung-up, and help us get beyond them and move on. This is done through understanding the basic drives, the voices of the conscience, the conditioning of the selves that make up the self. The point is not to strengthen the self, but to get out of its shackles.

## SKINNER — THE OUTER WORLD

B.F. Skinner is a psychologist whose concept of personality development is totally different from Freud's. Skinner and his followers are behaviorists. They believe that people are shaped not by inner agenda, but by outer environment entirely: the rewards and punishments of the outer world and other people. Skinnerians believe that animals and people are conditioned by rewards and punishments to behave in certain ways, and that when the pattern of outer environment changes, the person changes. Behaviorists talk only in terms of observable behavior patterns, not of unconscious needs. Behaviorists have done a lot of research with animals, notably rats, monkeys, and pigeons, and with electronic devices for stimuli, food for rewards. Animals were rewarded with food when they rang a bell properly, punished by withholding food when they did not. One of the major conclusions behaviorists arrived at is that reinforcing positive behavior with a reward works better than punishment for failure.

Behaviorism stresses, not biochemical, genetic heredity or developmental psychology, but environmental influences on behavioral development. In arguments about nature vs. nurture, behaviorists would vote for nurture every time.

In terms of therapy, what this means is that while cognitive therapists (the talking/thinking kind) help you to think your way into right behavior, behavioral therapists ask you to change your behavior, and the thinking changes will follow. They might say: act your way into right thinking, not think your way into right acting.

Behaviorism has had great impact on the treatment of phobias and obsessive-compulsive disorders, alcoholism and other addictions. To help someone get over the fear of leaving the house, in agoraphobia (a fear of open spaces), instead of analysis, the therapist will suggest short trips before long ones. The twelve-step programs so often helpful in treating alcoholics and drug addicts begin with "Don't drink and go to meetings," and "Don't pick up and go to meetings." The good feelings about being able to leave the house or stop washing your hands over and over, the good feelings about being clean and sober, and a whole new life ahead, are the reinforcements for the behavior changes.

In ordinary life, behaviorism is part of the basis for advertising. If an advertiser can get some teenagers to wear baggy jeans or high-top sneakers, others will — the reinforcement is peer approval, belonging, being cool. A celebrity seen in certain clothes will influence the buying behavior of millions.

## THE CULTURAL/SOCIOLOGICAL PSYCHOLOGY GROUP

There are many psychologists today who think biochemistry and childhood development may be important, but who feel the culture, society-at-large has the greatest influence on personality formation. (Again, we are not discussing clinical disorders here, but personalities.)

Race, ethnic background, gender expectations, class, caste, economic position, educational opportunities, and so forth, are felt to be the most important formative influences. Freud, brilliant as he was, knew nothing of women's psyches and said once, "Anatomy is destiny" — meaning a woman needs only a man, a kitchen, and children in a home, where she should be kept at all times. Don't laugh. Women are now believed to be able to leave the house now, but they still have to be careful about it.

## THE WORLD OF YOUR BODY

Neurobiologists, brain chemistry experts, geneticists, gland specialists, and other medical scientists, believe, as the ancients did, that physical and chemical processes of the body are the predominant cause of behavior patterns. Their work in creating behavior changes with shock therapy, brain surgery, drugs, among other methods, has been supremely valuable, especially in clinical disorders. Most psychologists and psychotherapists believe that there are physical components to all mental illness and even some personality disorders. This is especially true with schizophrenia and other psychotic disorders where there is a loss of contact with reality and disturbances like hallucinations and delusions.

Take anxiety, for example.

The work of geneticists has been invaluable, also. Think, for instance, of a family where one child is an optimist, another a worry-wart. A 1990's National Institutes of Health's study of 500 men compared specific genes in subjects' DNA with the results of a questionnaire that measured everyday anxiety and other personality traits (as opposed to serious clinical disorders) of the serotonin-transporter gene. A variant of this gene seems to dispose people who have it to feel insecure, depressed, anxious no matter how their everyday lives are going. A child gets one serotonin-transporter gene from each parent: depending on which variant is present, this seems to mean that you can inherit anxiety the same way you can curly hair.

Take eating too much.

It is thought by some medical researchers that brain chemicals influence appetite, predisposing some people towards moderation and others to require little, and some of us never to know when we've had enough of anything. The chemical of craving, neuropeptide Y, Hara Estroff Marano, former editor of *Psychology Today* magazine, said recently, appears to be the body's most potent appetite stimulator. This research may be the key to a safe way, in the form of a chemical that blocks neuropeptide Y, to stem the alarming tide of obesity in the United States. The epicenter of eating behavior seems to be a cluster of nerve cells in the hypothalamus, deep in a most ancient part of the human race's brain. So actually there is a neurochemical of nibbling! A rush of neuropeptide Y ups the appetite — anorexics develop high levels of it to induce them to eat!

Psychologists who subscribe to the idea that physical and chemical processes explain most of our behavior and form the basis for our inner thoughts and emotions often suggest that one day the right kind of pill or combination of pills will clear up a lot of the confusion over our confusions.

**The Whole Picture**
So. What do you think? Suppose your eating behavior (or drinking behavior, or skateboarding, surfing, or shopping behavior) is from hell. Why? Possible explanations:

1. Freudian: your oral stage was deprived of enough bottle/breast sucking

2. Skinnerian: you got food as reward, food withheld as punishment

3. Neuropsychologist: your brain chemistry is off

4. The cultural/sociologist group: your ethnic background/race/gender is showing and telling you whatever shape you're in, you're wrong

Do you:

1. do psychotherapy?

2. reward yourself for dieting, selling your skateboard, surfboard, sobering up from drugs, alcohol, shopping?

3. take a pill?

4. move into a different tribe that likes fat people? people who skate too much, surf too much, shop, and so forth? change your sex?

Or:

See that all of these influences are realistic, probable, and universal. Then, stop killing yourself and find another hobby.

# The Personal Psychology Group

## Sigmund Freud

The personal developmental psychology crowd owes an immense debt to the genius of Freud. His uncovering the unconscious mind, the impact of personal experience on the unconscious mind, and the discovery that it is our unconscious motives that drive much of our behavior, was an extraordinary contribution to the understanding of the human psyche.

But Freud was also a man of his time (late 19th-early 20th century), of his own Austrian-Jewish conditioning and attitudes, particularly about sex and women. Sex was more forbidden then in that society than now, so he noted that most of his patient's neuroses stemmed from early sexuality and sexual repression. Today, the sexual climate is freer, and psychologists are paying attention to other sources of problems, problems of identity (who and what am I? where am I going? where, if anywhere, do I belong?). In Freud's day, pretty much everyone had a place within the family and community, transportation did not include jets, and custom limited young people's travels anyway. Many psychological pressures were different then, though many remain the same.

But it wasn't just differences in pressures. There came to be differences in theory and observation of the formation of personality in those who came after Freud.

L ater psychologists like Erik Erikson believed people changed and experienced growth beyond early childhood (Freud believed that everything important to personality development happened in the first six years, though eventually he observed that adult experience could reverse or alter childhood trauma). Erikson stressed the importance of continuing growth and developmental stages in the individual throughout life. (In Freud's day, this was less evident because each generation did things a lot like the generations before; society did not change as swiftly as in this century.)

Psychologists today study the methods of nurturing children and understanding adolescence. In Freud's day, there was more discipline than understanding. The study of women and their problems is as recent as the women's liberation movement, the Second Wave of 1965-1975, and the Third Wave of the 1990's. Freud, sadly, as we have previously mentioned, understood almost nothing about women. He felt that women envied men their sex. We know today women envy men their freedom. He felt the only fulfillment for women was in housework and babies (a lot of nonsense since women need something of their own to do just as much as men in order to grow and fulfill their needs). But of course in Freud's day there were few jobs or careers for women, and no one talked about these things, so how could he find out that women get tired of slinging hash and saying, "there, there, dear."

Anyway, Freud did discover the importance of the unconscious in determining personality and behavior. He did discover that by getting people to talk about their thoughts, memories, feelings, and dreams, he could understand and help his patients to understand the roots of their problems and thereby free them to go on living their lives without being emotionally, and sometimes physically, crippled.

Freud started out in Vienna as a neurologist (a specialist in the nervous system) at a time when there was no known treatment for people who suffered physically for reasons that weren't physical. Freud experimented with hypnosis, but hypnosis seems to have only short-term effects.

The patients' symptoms returned, usually soon after the treatments stopped. Then one day a medical friend told Freud about a patient named Anna O. who, after talking about the first time she had experienced a particular symptom, suddenly stopped having the symptom. Freud seized the idea of the 'talking cure' and from it developed psychoanalysis. He had patients who suffered paralysis, fears of all kinds, problems in seeing, hearing, having sex — all sorts of symptoms whose basis lay not in their bodies, but in their minds. He had his patients lie comfortably on a couch while he sat out of sight behind their heads. He encouraged them to talk, with little or no interruption from himself, about anything at all that came into their heads. For many patients, the process brought understanding.

As Freud began to analyze his patients, in order to understand them better, he analyzed himself — an agonizing process of recreating his own childhood, facing his own painful feelings about his parents, despite the shame, the fear of confronting his own truths. And it was from this, and from his experience with other people's minds that he developed his knowledge of the unconscious: the developmental stages of early childhood, latency, adolescence; the defense mechanisms we use; the interpretations of dreams; the unconscious conflicts that pull us; the fact that often there is a meaning underlying little everyday mistakes; and that we do not say and do things by accident (like breaking an arm — do you crave attention? or calling someone by the wrong name — would you rather be talking to someone else?). No one until Freud really understand the importance of early childhood and that what happens to us then shapes our personalities — our conflicts, anxieties, accomplishments, failures, and emotional patterns for life.

Although Freud developed his theories and psychoanalytic technique primarily to treat patients with psychological disorders, he went beyond medical therapy to a conception of the general human personality, normal as well as abnormal psychology (though those phrases are not much used today).

And he had no easy time of it, introducing the idea that a child had an early sex life into a Victorian world. People were horrified then at the thought of infantile sexuality. Many still are.

Freud had three major disciples — Adler, Jung, and Rank — who learned from him and then one by one broke with him to add their own contributions to the new field of depth psychology. They are the four classic Western founders of the science of the self. Although it must be said that in the ancient Eastern world, among the Greeks, even during the European Renaissance, writers and philosophers knew of the hidden levels beneath consciousness, no one before had developed usable techniques for getting to those levels.

Perhaps it was because before then, tradition, family, social pattern, religion, rituals of all kinds kept people's heads together. After the Industrial Revolution in the nineteenth

century, these patterns began to fall apart, and people began to move away from their traditional homes and farms
and towns. They became loners, and had to look into themselves for meaning, having lost the crutches of custom and
tradition.

The understanding of the individual then became
necessary.

### Alfred Adler

And that is where Alfred Adler made a major contribution. Where Freud saw patterns of sexual and family conflict as the basis of neuroses, Adler thought in terms of individual psychology. Whereas Freud was an explorer after the
truth of human behavior by tracing slowly back to the roots
of personality in childhood, Adler stressed daily personal
interactions as the problems. He felt that the person with
personality disorders has trouble facing the daily difficulties of life and either retreats into fantasy or gets ill so that
things don't have to be faced.

The important practical difference was in the therapy technique. Instead of using long hours on the couch to delve
into a patient's past, Adler, with his intense desire to help
immediately, taught his patients to cope with the present.
Adler's theory was that people are driven by a basic need to
overcome their inferiority, that all children, being small and
weak, start out with a need to compensate, to accomplish,
that personality disorders are really cases of wounded van-
ity. From Adler we get the expression "inferiority complex."
Adler felt the task of psychology was less a matter of medi-

cally rooting out deep-seated problems, than of replacing moral values, and that society's problem was competitive individualism. There are many therapists today whose technique derives both from Freud and Adler — part tracing back to the patient's past, part helping the patient to cope with daily life, a combination of "depth" and "here-and-now" psychology.

## Carl Jung

Carl Jung also broke away from Freud and founded the school of "analytic psychology," a description that doesn't make much sense since this whole business is analytical. At any rate, Jung broadened the understanding of the psyche to include not only the Personal Unconscious but the Collective Unconscious, the sum of the experience of the human race. In other words, he understood that not only does your psyche contain your own past, but elements of society's past all the way back through time. Whatever our individual differences, said Jung, we all share certain racial experiences. And we all share spiritual yearning, for god and the universe.

Jung's understanding of personality is that it is linked to archeology, literature, myth, and history as well as psychology. He said that the libido is general psychic energy, not just sexual energy as Freud had said, and that this energy works in four ways: thinking, feeling, intuition, sensation. Jung divided people into types, depending on which of the four movements was strongest. And also on whether a person was introverted or extroverted, outward-going or inward. A balance of all these qualities, he said, is necessary for a healthy personality. Too much or too little of any of these functions creates personality disturbance.

Jung felt the Personal Unconscious was important with its basic drives, personal experience, conscience, but he also felt that the Collective Unconscious provides us with inborn patterns of behavior (like birds who are born knowing exactly how to build their nests or fly south), especially in the areas of myth and religion and spirituality. Jung called these patterns archetypes, and while he felt that the instincts supply our energy, our inborn images — archetypes (universal symbols inside all of us) — give us the inspiration toward a more meaningful life. Jung's concept of the Self begins with the idea that self-development is a lifelong process in a human being, in which one's potential for wholeness and for creativity is unconsciously realized, and that we must reach beyond ourselves to fulfill the Self.

Jung's awareness of our essential loneliness, the need to confront our inner natures and reach our creative potential in order to overcome that loneliness, was as much a part of his therapy as the origins of neurotic symptoms.

## Otto Rank

Otto Rank was the third great disciple of Freud. Rank broke with Freud over the concept of the basic personality drive. To Rank, it was not sexual and aggressive drives, but the Will (like Jung's Self, unconscious). The Will is the instinctual force by which a human being emerges as an individual; it is the inner principle of the psyche, the power by which we separate ourselves from one another. Rank saw the shock of birth as the major trauma, the anxiety of separation from the mother, which causes separation anxiety all our lives, the fear of being alone. Counteracting that fear, and the need to be part of others, the Will fights to make sure we stay separate, stay individuals. This fight against others, Rank believed, is what produces guilt; and coping with that guilt, in life or therapy, makes a healthy person. Rank also added to Freud's basic drives the "urge toward immortality," a driving force inside us that produces art, religion, civilization, children — all the [so-called] creative things the human race has accomplished. Rank felt we have to go beyond psychology of the individual, to broaden our concept of personality toward the concept of the supernatural as well.

Freud and Adler, basically, were concerned with individual psyches. Jung and Rank were more interested in the impersonal foundations of our personalities. From the medical-analytical to the spiritual, the four men laid the basis for psychology today.

### Next Generation

There have been many followers of these four great men who have further broadened the field of psychology as they sought to cope with a changing world, who have found new ways to study human behavior and new techniques to help people.

Karen Horney, Harry Stack Sullivan, Erich Fromm, Erik Erikson, Peter Blos, Helene Deutsch, Eric Berne, and many others. Peter Blos has done good work in the area of adolescent psychology. Erik Erikson has developed studies of the social significance of childhood and the relationship of different cultures to the development of a child's personality. Fromm's field is studying people's ability to develop their hidden capacities for love, in that they are social animals and their satisfactions are socially based. Karen Horney's work comes from her belief that the personality develops from having to adapt to life, that a prime motivating factor in personality is the need for security, and she has contributed a great deal to the psychology of women, as has Helene Deutsch. Harry Stack Sullivan believed in interpersonal relationships as the basis of personality, that if a child's early experiences were good and the child felt good about itself, all went well. Otherwise, not the "good me" but the "bad me" develops along with a whole lot of anxiety. (Or even the "not me," which leads to psychopathology.) Unlike Freud, who found psychotics difficult and too self-absorbed for psychoanalysis, Sullivan believed we discover nothing new in those with mental illness — only the deeper layers of ourselves laid bare. For Sullivan, it was the early transactions between child and parents that determines mental states.

Gestalt Therapy is among the holistic approaches to therapy. Fritz Perls felt that mental illness arises when the individual interrupts the ongoing flow of life because of too much unfinished business that the process of living cannot go on. Perls preferred the here-and-now kind of therapy: if you can see what you are doing now, you will not only be able to understand your past, but change your behavior. The word gestalt is simply "the whole picture," and to look at the whole picture allows us to understand ourselves and our relationship to others.

## Group Therapists

Eric Berne's 1967 book *Games People Play* made transactional analysis (TA for short) very popular. It is conducted not between one therapist and one client (although a little of that goes on), but in group therapy with a trained facilitator. TA is based on the theory that all children are programmed by their parents to live out certain lifetime scripts and that if a script is self-destructive it can be changed by finding out what the script is and reprogramming a person's responses to situations and other people. The shift here is away from what goes on inside people to what goes on between people, away from inner conflict to external circumstances.

Berne's basic belief is that everyone is okay and can be "cured," that most people operate from "I'm not okay, you're okay," or "I'm okay, you're not okay," or "I'm not okay, you're not okay" positions. For emotional health, people must take the "I'm okay, you're okay" position. It's his belief that everybody, those with personality disorders, even those with clinical disorders, can be taught this, that everybody can be "cured." This staggers many people, but TA can be an eye-opener as to how people are programmed to inter-relate.

Berne felt the language of psychology should be simple so that everyone could understand it easily. Berne used the words Parent, Adult. Child for states of consciousness. He said these can be understood by listening to people interact with each other. The Parent, Adult, and Child voices in everybody's heads have their proper place, but unfortunately we don't always use them when we should and therefore we ruin our relationships, work situations, and family lives by bad transactions. This is because many people have been given a tragic blueprint in childhood and spend their lives trying to fight that blueprint instead of escaping the script altogether. Without help, unless they have the capacity to listen to themselves and change on their own, they never break out of their scripts, and they go on reliving the same unhappy situations over and over.

Parents can give their children a go-ahead-and-be-happy script to flower, or they can apply so many "don'ts" (don't touch the flowers=don't explore your senses; don't touch yourself=sex is bad and so are you if you like it; don't bother me all the time=intimacy is dangerous, your feelings get hurt if you try it — and so forth) that the child grows up cut off from his or her own feelings and everybody else's. Parents can program their children to be failures or successes, drunks or corporation presidents, to be happy living good lives or to be ruthless.

And this is when Berne talks about the *Games People Play*. Everyone needs strokes of warmth and recognition. All people need attention. And if people can't get positive strokes, they would rather settle for negative strokes than no strokes at all. The Child in all of us needs intimacy, but intimacy is so threatening (scary, full of emotional problems and responsibilities a lot of people can't handle because they have been taught to panic at psychic nakedness) that we play games instead with words. That way we can get our strokes without being too exposed. Instead of communicating directly, people get secret psychic payoffs from crossed transactions. Like this chart:

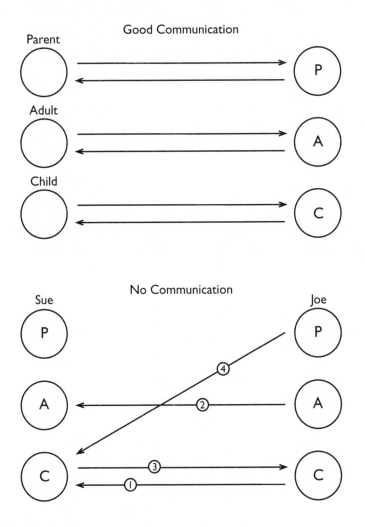

This is Berne's way of diagramming transactions. Transactions work well between people when Adult answers Adult in a conversation, Child answers Child, Parent answers Parent. When the Parent voice of one person answers the Child voice of another, there is a crossed transaction, which not only interrupts real communication but is an essential part of games. Parent is the voice of authority, judgment, morals. Adult is the voice of reality. Child is the voice of spontaneity, intimacy, creativity, emotional need and basic drives, joy, sex, pleasure.

SUE:    Do you love me, Joe? (*Sue's Child to Joe's Child*)

JOE:    Love is a big responsibility. (*Joe's Adult to Sue's Adult*)

This is a crossed transaction. The Child in Sue wants love, intimacy. The Adult in Joe, not the corresponding Child, has put Sue off. She has one of two choices. She can either come on Adult like Joe and discuss their feelings objectively, or, if she is desperate for a stroke, for warmth, she can play a game to see if she can get that stroke. What she does will depend on how her life script reads, how her parents gave or didn't give her love, how she learned to get their love, whether she feels okay about herself and thinks she deserves love, or not okay about herself and has to wheedle love or play games to get it.

SUE:    I love you, Joe. (*Could be Adult — simple fact —* or Child, depends on what comes next.)

JOE:     We're too young to be in love. *(Parent voice, judg-mental, speaking to Sue's Child.)*

SUE:     Oh, Joe, please, we're not too young to feel the way we do about each other. Love me, Joe. Love me. *(Child still reaching for joy and love in another Child.)*

JOE:     *(Exploding)* Stop pushing me, Sue. I'm just not ready for all that yet.

Sue got her stroke all right, from Joe's angry Child. But by pushing so hard, she was risking a negative stroke. Obviously, for Sue, any stroke was better than none, which comes from an "I'm not okay" position. She was playing a game to get her stroke, and the payoff was the kick in the head she got from Joe. Berne labeled the *Games People Play*, and this one he called Kick Me. People who have been handed life scripts that include rejection and punishment play the game a lot. The whole point to playing games is the payoff that people secretly need, whether it is good for them or not. In Sue's case, the payoff was to confirm her feelings that she is unlovable.

Berne's point is that instead of communicating honestly and openly with each other, we play games to satisfy unrecognized psychic goals. Sue, programmed differently, instead of desperately reaching for Joe's Child, might have been able to use her own Adult voice to say to Joe that she felt insecure, but that if Joe wasn't ready yet, she could wait for the word "love." Joe might have been less frightened with less pressure.

Games can often be played in which words sound one way but are loaded with hidden meanings. This allows people to get what they want from each other without having to ask openly for strokes. Yes, But is a popular game.

JANICE:    *(Nobody has been paying enough attention to her over lunch when their crowd met at the diner)* I'm so bored lately.

SHARYN:    I found a new dance teacher. Come with me on Saturday and work it off. It's so fun.

JANICE:    Yes, but I'm not coordinated like you.

VIRGINIA:    Well, how about learning keyboard with me?

JANICE:    Yes, but my father couldn't stand the noise.

SHARYN:    What about my computer class. Or even a part time job?

JANICE:    Yes, but...

And on it goes. The words seem to mean that Janice wants advice. Only she never takes any advice. What she wants are strokes, attention, and she doesn't know how to get it openly. So she plays Yes, But as long as people will play. They respond with Adult to her Child until they get tired of it and then come on with Parent, to end the transaction. "You sure have a problem, and you'd better do something about it." Or, if the other person is also playing a game like enjoying the role of rescuing Parent, it can go on for years, with two people having a P-C relationship forever and never really communicating with each other at all.

Having been given patterns of responses by their parents, people go on responding and behaving in the same way all their lives. It works out if your parents have given you permission to be okay, to work and relate well to others. It works out badly if your mother keeps telling you you're going to be a drunk like your Uncle Harry, or you're a bad kid and no one will ever love you, or you better love taking care of others or you'll never be a woman, or if you don't like to play football you're not a real man. Stuff like that makes people feel like Frogs instead of Princes and Princesses, Berne's followers say.

TA therapy is one of the group therapies that works with the here and now, the daily responses to immediate problems, rather than in terms of sorting out the past conflicts that caused present problems. In this kind of therapy, it's less important why you have a script than what the script is and how to change it. Berne implies that a script-free person whose Adult can cope with situations clearly is a healthy person. Those whose Parent and Child voices constantly interfere with their behavior and order them about have problems. It's hard to get through life if a voice in your head is constantly telling you you're a louse, a drunk, a failure. And it's hard to get through life if you're constantly behaving like a needy Child. Some Parent judgment is necessary. The joy and spontaneity of your Child is necessary. But your Adult should know when and where. And your Adult should be able to respond where an Adult voice is called for:

MY DAUGHTER:    *(Adult)* Mom, which way do you like my hair, this way or this?

ME:                     *(Coming on Parent)* I asked you to clean up your room this morning and it's still a mess.

MY DAUGHTER:    *(Patiently still Adult)* I'll clean my room in five minutes. I p r o m i s e . But I have a date tonight and I need to know about my hair. So could you stop coming on Parent just a minute?

I have one of three choices. I can still come on Parent and order her to clean her room. I can come on Child and be furious at being frustrated. Or I can have a real moment of communication with my daughter and say, "You're right. The way you look tonight is more important. Let's do your hair." My response will depend on how I've been programmed as a child.

The TA people say there are three ways lives get distorted into scripts.

1. Without love, there come depression scripts.

2. If your parents haven't allowed you to use your own mind (they've made all your decisions, negated your sense of reality, etc.), then there are madness scripts.

3. Without joy, there come drug addiction scripts.

TA people feel that diagnosis of your script, followed by permission (given by group therapy leader or others in the group, or friends) to stop following it will allow you to change your behavior. Once again, there is the understanding that insight is the factor of change, not the force of will.

These, then, are the followers of Freud, the men and women who believe behavior is determined by inner forces, even if some of them hold that external forces beyond the early years influence those inner forces.

Next, the totally external approach.

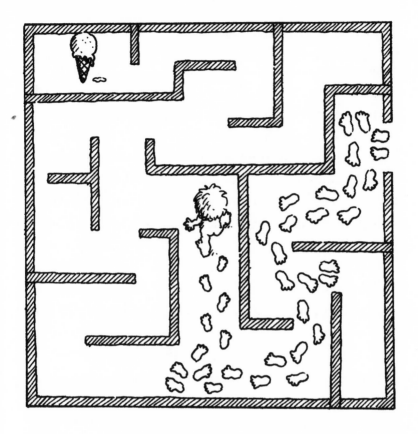

# The Behaviorists

B F. Skinner and his group believe that all human beings
are alike and can be conditioned to behave in predict-
able ways.

Skinner's theory is that your environment — the people,
places, and things around you — shapes your behavior, and
that if your environment is changed, your behavior will
change. Skinner's group rejects the exploration of your unconscious, your inner feelings, as unscientific. The focus of

treatment, if you're in trouble, is not on you, but on changing the way people handle you. They believe that rewards and punishments make you behave as you do, and that rewards condition behavior better than punishments. Since "bad" behavior has been learned by external conditioning (slaps, smiles, approval or disapproval from the people around you), it can be unlearned — not by finding out how you feel inside and why — but by changing what's going on outside you instead.

Like this.

Jerry has been an attention-getter all his life, sometimes with constructive behavior, sometimes destructive. When he was small, it was mostly constructive. He put on shows for his parents, clowning to amuse them, or did the dishes for his mother, or learned how to handle a tool to surprise his father. At seven or eight he got straight A's in school and was better than anyone on a skateboard. Along with some of this positive behavior went sudden temper tantrums, and occasional disappearances when he was supposed to be somewhere.

Now, at the age of thirteen, suddenly Jerry's behavior has become very negative. He is late for classes at school, disrupts the class by fighting or shouting questions that have nothing to do with the subject, starts arguments that get teammates into trouble or shows up out of uniform at basketball practice, and some girls have complained about being grabbed. He has been accused of petty theft. He has been caught smoking dope. At home, he is late for dinner or won't eat. He either argues or remains sullen.

His teachers have had it, his friends won't talk to him, his parents are losing their minds. Help is necessary.

*Jerry's parents could put him into ordinary therapy, during which Jerry's inner conflicts would be explored. Jerry might possibly discover that he has a deep belief that he is unworthy of love, that he has to perform in order to get love and attention, that this makes him angry. And so instead of performing well, he now makes his performances punitive toward himself and everyone else, especially his parents, since he is still overly dependent on their love and is fighting this dependency by negative behavior. He would perhaps gain insight into all the reasons for these things and learn that he is worthy of love without having to be a performing seal all the time, positively or negatively.*

Jerry's parents chose the behaviorist method instead, and Jerry's whole environment was changed to restructure his behavior. Whatever Jerry did from then on, he got a different reaction from any he had ever had before.

A behavioral psychologist was called in to meet with Jerry's parents and teachers, and a "contract" was drawn. Jerry can do whatever he wants, but everybody else has to behave differently from the way they would have before. Simply stated, if Jerry misbehaves, he is to be ignored. Not punished, just sent away from the group, class, sports, the dinner table, whatever. Before, Jerry was rewarded by attention for bad behavior, even if the attention was angry. Now, he is simply to be left out. No one will question him, comfort him, ask about his feelings. If he wants to cooperate again, the usual rewards for good behavior will be there. If he doesn't want to cooperate, he goes it alone. In this restructured environment both at school and at home, there is to be no pay-off in attention for bad behavior.

The behaviorist will warn Jerry's parents that if the "contract" is removed, Jerry's "bad" behavior may return. If it does, the "contract" has to be used again. And again. Until after a while Jerry understands that "good" behavior is rewarding and "bad" behavior isn't, even when the contract is removed.

**The Skinner Box**

This conditioning process was begun by Skinner with animals and birds. Using a "Skinner box," behaviorists put a rat inside. There is a lever in the box that, when pressed, produces food. After a few accidental bumps that produce the food, the rat learns to press the lever on purpose when it is hungry. The rat has become "conditioned" to expect a reward for behaving the way the scientist wants to it to behave. Skinner also experimented with punitive shocks to condition behavior, but he discovered good behavior had fewer relapses when it was rewarded than when bad behavior was punished. After a lot of experiments with animals and birds, Skinner decided the same system could apply to people. No one asked how the rat felt, and it behaved. Maybe it could be true of people, too. He relied only on observable fact, never on inner abstracts.,

**The Reward System**

Skinnerians have been doing work in mental wards trying to improve the behavior of people with mental illness and even people with mental retardation. They try to reinforce good behavior (getting the clients to eat, communicate, do recreational therapy, keep themselves clean, respond in healthier ways) by rewards, and improve "bad" behavior by withholding rewards.

The behaviorist approach conditions not just "good" and "bad" but functional or healthy behavior vs. dysfunctional, harmful, or unhealthy behavior. A woman with mental illness is too disturbed to care about keeping herself clean. Coaxing and help in grooming reinforce the "bad" behavior because the woman gets attention. Skinner would advise, pay no attention to the patient or remove a privilege, but if she does clean herself up, give her a reward. (She may watch television again, whatever.)

A man with clinical depression wants to remain alone, in bed, to sleep away the day. Even if he is coaxed out of bed, he sits in a corner to maintain his privacy because he is too miserable to join the group. Skinner might advise, condition his behavior by disapproval rather than special attention. Do not permit special food or privileges.

Take one more example. Two children grow up in the same house with the same parents, are sent to the same schools, have the same advantages. One takes advantage of all this and turns out fine. The other messes up. Most developmental psychologists, neuropsychologists, geneticists, would say that everybody responds slightly differently even in the same environment depending on their personal perceptions, nervous systems, genetic makeup. A Skinnerian might have the parents withhold rewards from the second child until it developed responsibility, shaped up (or shipped out?) on the grounds that all people are the same, respond similarly to similar stimuli, and just need proper "conditioning."

Many ethical and moral questions have been raised about behaviorists. The most important question has to do with those in control! Who decides what behavior is acceptable? Who has the right to reinforce a certain kind of behavior? On the one hand, behavioral therapy is the only known non-pharmacologically effective treatment for phobias and obsessive-compulsive disorders. On the other hand, it can deprive the young, the weak, the sick, the helpless, of so much free will that they cannot even protest by behaving differently, often their only means of crying for help. There is the suggestion in behaviorist theory of a kind of psychological dictatorship that makes many people uncomfortable.

"As the twig is bent, so grows the tree," is an old saying. But old sayings and advertising-run media, government propaganda and scientific/medical pronouncements need inquiry.

Bending a twig, selling a sneaker, and behavioral therapy or enforcement only go so far to change people. In the long run, external reinforcement may not always work. A molested child will not always turn out to be a molester. A child treated generously may not always turn into a Santa Claus.

In the famous case of John-Joan, when the genital surgery performed on the boy baby's deformed genitals turned him from boy to girl, and he was brought up a girl, reinforced as a girl, dressed as a girl, he still felt like a boy and took the first surgical opportunity to turn himself back into the male he had always been.

Nature cannot be ignored. A baby's brain is not a blank slate on which you can just write whatever you want. Clearly both nature and nurture are at work in the formation of personality.

Even on the grand scale, behavioralism may not even work. For 10,000 years or more, governmental revolutions have been based on the theory that if you just change the external environment, people will be better off. And we're still at war, many still live in poverty and without education or any other way out of their misery.

Real change seems to be an inner, not an external, job.

And what causes real change seems to be insight and understanding, not force.

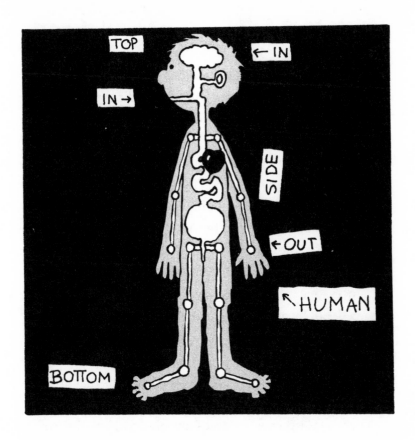

# The Body People

The personal experience psychologists, cognitive psychologists, examine inner mental and emotional states to explain behavior.

Behaviorists like Skinner think environment shapes our behavior.

Biopsychologists, neurobiologists, brain chemists, and scientists in many fields related to neuropsychology explain behavior and even feelings in terms of brain chemistry.

Advanced technology now includes the use of neurophysiological testing; electrophysiological recording; and brain imaging. Neurophysiological tests examine dysfunctions in the nervous system that may relate to mental illnesses such as schizophrenia, obsessive-compulsive disorders, mood disorders, and anxiety disorders. These scientists relate strongly to specialists in artificial intelligence, to consider our personalities almost purely in terms of the material brain in a material body. In short, they look at us as we might consider a computer. These scientists feel that the body's electrochemical processes explain our behavior and that behavior can be changed, not by altering the environment or understanding our selves, but by altering the body.

There are mild therapies in this field like hydrotherapy — water therapy — warm or ice-packed baths that are supposed to soothe or numb the body and therefore the mind.

There are stronger therapies like electroshock therapy in which electric currents are sent through the brain to the whole nervous system. This therapy is sometimes used on withdrawn, depressed, suicidal patients to make them "open up" for psychoanalytical therapy. The treatment produces a series of convulsions, and because it has sometimes been used indiscriminately in institutions or as punishment for bad behavior, many states are beginning to restrain its use.

But the two hottest areas in this field, and the ones over which there has been the most argument, are brain surgery and chemotherapy (drugs).

## Brain Surgery

*Phillip seemed to be a perfectly okay kid (except for being slow at schoolwork and perception) until at the age of eighteen he suddenly began to have fits of violence. At first, his rages were just a matter of throwing and breaking things. Then one day, in a fury at what he thought was an insulting remark from a classmate, Phillip threw the boy to the ground and stabbed him with a penknife. A couple of months later, when his mother asked Phillip to set the kitchen table for dinner, Phillip flew into a rage, grabbed a kitchen knife and stabbed his mother's arm.*

*Something had to be done about Phillip. He was put in a mental institution where analysis, drugs, electroshock therapy were all tried. Nothing stopped Phillip's sudden violent seizures. Finally, a brain surgeon talked to Phillip's parents.*

*The brain surgeon said there were three possibilities:*

1. *Phillip could be kept in an institution the rest of his life under constant supervision.*

2. *A prefrontal lobotomy could be performed, an operation on the front part of the brain which severs nerve connections. This operation would completely eradicate the violence, but it would also erase Phillip's ability to think. He would become a walking vegetable. The operation, once overly used in violent cases, was seldom used any more, the surgeon explained.*

3. *By using an EEG machine, they could test for abnormal electrical activity in Phillip's brain, locate where the abnormal electrical discharge patterns came from, and destroy those brain cells with an electrode.*

Phillip's parents were horrified both at lifelong institutionalization and at the idea of turning Phillip into a totally helpless vegetable. It was chancey (both because the full effects on behavior and the future side effects of brain surgery are still unknown and because there are still not enough studies and follow-ups to know whether such procedures work on a long-term basis). Phillip's parents chose the brain surgeon's third suggestion. After the operation, Phillip will live at home instead of in an institution. Supposedly, though the seizures will still recur occasionally, they will be controllable in the future with drugs. The surgery will not change the original psychotic disorder that caused Phillip's slowness and rage, but it is possible he can lead a semi-normal life.

## Drugs

*Dana was a young writer. For many years she had suffered from a mood disorder, manic-depression. Not severely enough to be put in a hospital, but enough to make her personal life increasingly impossible. Her illness meant that she suffered from mood swings that were driving her up walls. For months she would be so depressed she could hardly get out of bed, much less work or enjoy her children. Then something marvelous would happen. Her mood would change, she would fall in love or write and sell another book, and she'd be on top of the world. But it wasn't an ordinary happiness, it was a crazy sort of high, during which she'd spend too much money, talk too much, make idiotic decisions, adore someone so much she'd nearly drive him crazy, too. Then eventually she'd lose the lover or mess up the book she was writing, get depressed, and the whole pattern would start all over again.*

*Dana went into psychotherapy. It was important to uncover the conflicts that made her so desperate for attention and success that she went to pieces without them, and to find out why, when she got them, she couldn't handle them properly. Her psychiatrist was very helpful. But he knew that more than talk was necessary, he knew her brain chemistry was imbalanced, and he prescribed drugs to even out the highs and elevate the lows so that her moods were less painful and her life was more stabilized.*

*Then came the problem of possible side effects. Maybe the depression would be helped by certain drugs, but would she be too spaced out to write? A number of artists he had treated complained that the drugs turned them into cows and they couldn't work. Dana was tried on a number of drugs for the highs, the lows, and her anxiety disorder as well. Her manicky, what she called her "flying" moods leveled, the lows were not bovine, and her anxieties lessened. The drugs are working, for now. She can work. More important, she has enough chemical tranquility to examine more deeply her inner life.*

There are many people like Dana with many kinds of psychotic, personality, dissociative, and anxiety disorders, both inside and outside of hospitals, who seem to have benefited by changing the body chemistry by drugs. There are also learning disabilities and attention deficit disorders that seem to be helped with drugs. The major consideration is still that though these drugs seem to work, the reasons why they work isn't always certain and the long-range results of altering behavior by altering the physical self alone — its chemistry, brain cell transmitters, it metabolism — are still debatable. This group of scientists argue their worth on the grounds that they just seem to work, at least for the present.

### Genetics

Geneticists as well as neurobiologists and brain chemists are aware that we are all born with differing DNA elements, different genetic equipment, which accounts for differences in our behavior not caused by childhood experiences or environment. We all have slightly different nervous systems, stomachs, hearts, predispositions toward this or that disease, and so forth. While they agree that upbringing is an important influence, they feel that it is our physical selves that make us react to that environment (as in two children reacting differently to the same parents). Geneticists are discovering increasingly often, that certain kinds of mental illness are due, at least in part, to genetic makeup rather than only to environmental factors. It seems we inherit, along with long legs or lovely ears, inborn gifts like music ability and IQ. We also inherit physical, chemical, genetic errors, of metabolism, of mood, of chemical balances that have nothing to do with parental or societal influence on a young child.

Genes and the DNA they contain modulate how one responds to environment. Dean Hamer, a molecular biologist and psychologist who works in a lab at the National Institutes of Health, says we inherit, for instance, a biological predisposition to cheerfulness, or to depression. This is actually measurable, because EEG machines indicate smilers, people with enthusiasm, people who report being happy most of the time, have more left frontal activity than those who are depressed. It was Hamer and his colleagues whose studies linked anxiety and depression, hostility and impulsiveness to a gene involved in the production of serotonin, the brain chemical affected by Prozac, just as enthusiasm was linked to the brain's response to dopamine. With 100,000 genes along the human genome, Hamer feels 30% to 70% of the human personality and behavior is regulated by inherited genes. In a 1997 *Discover* magazine article, Hamer adds, genes are not a neurobiological and behavioral destiny. Nor are we at the mercy of environment, parents, teachers, and every TV movie. The seat of behavior is the brain, and the influences on the brain are many and complex.

## Biofeedback

Biofeedback training is another new area in the physical approach to psychology.

Suppose you have a lot of physical symptoms you know result from tension and anxiety. Like before an exam your neck aches, your stomach hurts, your legs cramp up. Not just once in a while, but every time you face some kind of emotional stress you get certain physical symptoms. This happens because certain messages are sent to the part of your brain you have no voluntary control over, the part that controls breathing, heart rate, muscle tension, and so forth.

You can be taught by a specialist in psychosomatic (conversion of mental into physical symptoms) medicine how the mind affects the body, how to pay attention to body symptoms caused by stress, and how to relax those muscles before they cause you lower back pain, severe headaches, and so forth. Pain, or illness, caused by stress is very real. The brain's stress chemicals can make real trouble, from sciatica nerve pain to heart attacks.

There is great debate, rightly, about brain surgery, the long-term effects of certain drugs. After all, brain surgery can't be undone, and even if certain drugs help improve behavior, the future side effects on the body are in many cases still unknown.

But with all the debate, there is no question of the value of research on the influence of the body, including the brain, on the mind states. There are physical causes for some mental illnesses. There are mental causes for some physical illnesses.

Even before I knew anything about psychology, I had a hunch that Shakespeare probably had a good stomach and digestive system. Based solely on the fact that I have never been able to write when I was nauseous.

How many people could be more productive or lead fuller lives if by altering their electrical-chemical selves they could also alter their behavior, avoid stress, and conquer pain? The body people have a point. If you are physically healthy and chemically balanced, your mind has a better chance of functioning well. A rider doesn't get far on a lame horse or on a motorcycle with its cylinders out of whack.

# A Few More

There are a few more approaches to the causes for an improvement of human behavior that need to be mentioned.

**The Sociocultural Approach**

The psychologists in this field do not focus on a patient's behavior, inner conflicts, defense mechanisms, or even biochemistry. They focus instead on the influence of the community, the social and cultural setting from which the client came. They feel that these wider forces shape human lives and behavior, both for good and bad, rather than more personal forces. These psychologists have formed social-action research groups, preventive community programs, therapeutic hospital communities.

When this new movement first started in the 1960's, it received a lot of government help — probably because it seemed simpler to clear up a whole lot of psyches all at once by simply blaming everything on the street a person happened to grow up on. There is no question but that class, money, education, the amount of crime around, cultural pursuits, traditions, rats in your kitchen or flowers in your garden influence your personality. But there is also a great deal of question as to whether that's all there is to it. If cultural influence alone creates behavior patterns, how come kids who have every "advantage" turn into drug dealers and kids who have had no advantages become bank presidents?

There are excellent psychologists today like Michael Riera (*Surviving High School*, 1997), Mary Pipher (*Reviving Ophelia*, 1994), Peggy Orenstein (*School Girls*, 1994) who combine personal development psychology and sociocultural psychology to give a more complete picture of the way our minds are conditioned.

## Reality Therapy

William Glasser felt that mental illness simply did not exist and created a here-and-now therapy to deal with the problems of daily living: the need to love and be loved, the need to feel worthwhile to oneself and other people. He felt a therapist could teach a client to meet those two basic needs within the framework of her or his daily "reality." Since we all carry our entire past around in our heads, just how do we behave "here and now" as if nothing that happened to us before matters — this is one major objection to Glasser. There are people walking around who devote their entire lives to an absolute and stubborn crusade: NEVER LET THE FAMILY OFF THE HOOK, NEVER FORGET THE HUNDRED MILLION AFFRONTS SUFFERED UNTIL THE END OF TIME. This is part of the victim psychology (it's everybody's else's fault I committed the crime, not mine) in the courts today. What Glasser might say is, stick to a simpler explanation than delving into past pathologies. Sometimes a sociopath is just a sociopath.

The point is, though, emotionally ill people are hung up in their past, which is part of their psychic reality, and they cannot simply be taught to rearrange their daily behavior.

### Gesell, Spock, Piaget

Dr. Arnold Gesell founded and directed the Clinic of Child Development at Yale University in 1911. He was a pioneer in systematic recorded studies of child growth and behavior, tracing the behavior patterns and characteristics of children at every age and stage of growth and development, and interpreting them in terms of parental, school, and community influence.

His underlying concepts are developmental, and his advice is basically a mixture of interpersonal relationship psychology and environmental structure. His books on child development and child guidance through every sneeze and temper tantrum have had an immense practical value for parents and teachers, who can find out from Gesell quickly and easily that it's perfectly normal for a two-and-a-half-year-old child to say "no" to you twenty-four hours a day and at another stage and age, in the teens, say nothing to you at all. Gesell has made an enormous contribution — having interviewed millions of children — to the study of average patterns of growth, and the characteristic behavior of children and their responses. His books help both young people and parents understand average behavior patterns. It must, of course, be remembered that this is a statistical approach, a set of averages. So if and when you read Gesell, don't panic if you find your characteristics belong one-third to an eight-year-old, one-third to a ten-year-old, one-third to an eighteen-year-old — and you happen to be fourteen-and-a-half.

Dr. Benjamin Spock's *Baby and Child Care* influenced so many of your grandparents and therefore your parents, that a look at it might tell you a lot about your upbringing. Discipline and spoiling, how your sleep problems were handled, what adults did about the physical and psychological care of their young in the first half of this century.

Jean Piaget remains a great name in the field of research. His studies were in child psychology, particularly in developmental learning stages, the development of intellect and adaptive intelligence at different stages of a child's growth and experience.

Historically, then, these were the three main approaches to the understanding of human behavior—the developmental approach, the behaviorist approach, the body approach. Each has something very important to contribute, as does the cultural approach, the statistical approach, the IQ capability approach.

**Other Scientists**

*Consciousness Explained*, 1991, by Daniel Dennett is an excellent science book that explores the nature of consciousness, artificial intelligence, neurobiology, cognitive psychology in a search to understand the mind-brain.

He talks about the many information centers in the brain, the absence of a single ghost in the machine, or some tiny homunculus in there directing traffic. As he says, no matter how hard you look in there, you'll find nobody home. You'll find the same thing in your brain as you find in the rest of the universe if you look for it — life, intelligence.

*Wholeness and the Implicate Order*, 1980, by David Bohm is a complicated book by a quantum physicist and metaphysical philosopher. He writes about the whole reflected in every part and every part reflecting the whole. He writes about the observer affecting everything observed. When you look at something, you change it in some way.

Even more important, however, than that the scientists understand you, is that you understand you. What follows are the teachings of someone who can help you to do your own understanding on your own.

# The Joy Of Freedom

In case you haven't figured out yet what this whole book is leading up to, what the whole point of understanding your nature, the nature of your mind, is all about, it's the joy of freedom. By this is meant not just physical freedom (you may have to work very hard, long physical hours in your life), but psychological freedom.

The meaning of life is life itself, living itself, and you can't live life fully and freely if you are locked inside the prison of your mind. Krishnamurti, or just K, as he called himself, was dedicated to setting human beings free from their mental suffering. His teachings, his insights show us that most of our suffering is created by all the thoughts and feelings, prejudices and political and personal fears that have been stuffed into us for thousands of years. What he said was, it isn't a description of freedom that will set us free, but learning how to break down what creates the prison. The way to do this is to question everything that governs your behavior. Examine your self-images, your prejudices. Pay attention to your behavior in relationships. We must move on from just saying the politically correct things and actually change our human nature.          ♦

Krishnamurti left India as a boy. He gave talks and held dialogues in many countries all over the world for sixty years. He was much loved as teacher and spiritual philosopher. He talked with students as well as teachers, farmers as well as professors. He did not think insight was only for the educated. His insights into the nature of the self, thought, suffering, meditation, sex, love, the mysteries of life and death, the sacred and human consciousness influenced some of the greatest thinkers of our time. The essence of his message in all the years he taught remained essentially the same: each of us represents all humanity, and each one needs to be a light to oneself, free of all psychological authority. Just as we question received opinion in science, we must question it morally and psychologically.

He taught and founded schools in the United States, England, and India — he knew it was as important for kids to understand their own brains and how to live their lives as to make a living.

He held talks at the United Nations, with the Dalai Lama, with scientists, doctors, writers, and with heads of state. He had no interest in theories. He only taught people to think clearly for themselves, not according to other people's ideas, and without relying psychologically on authority. The world tells you what to do and what not to do, but they don't tell you how to find out for yourself what is true!

K said "Truth is a pathless land."

What he meant was:

1. You can't find out about the truths of your life by following leaders or through organizations. Each one must discover what is true and sacred for oneself.

2. You can find the truth in the mirror of relationships. By the mirror of relationship is meant: you can see what you are in the way you relate to people. Observe your reactions and responses. For instance, do you turn others into approval-givers, try to dominate and control them, try to get them to take care of you? Do you turn others into parents, best friends, brothers, sisters, try to possess them, or push them away when they get too close? Do you give to get? Or just because? Are you cruel or kind? Also, how do you relate to work, to school, to parents, teachers, god, country, strangers?

3. Understand that you can only know yourself and others in the present, not through the memory of yesterday, but through paying attention today. Even our past is better understood by paying attention to how you are thinking and behaving *right now*. We change less than we think.

4. Understand your own conditioning, the contents of your mind, the thoughts, fears, angers, ambitions, likes, dislikes, memories, experiences. Don't let these dictate your actions, your behavior. Joy lies in the freedom from all the contents and images and prejudices of our consciousness that keep hanging us up.

K points out that we keep creating images to give our selves a sense of security. It makes us feel as if we belong. Whether these images are political, religious, or personal images (I am this, I am that, you have to be this, you aren't that) they dominate our thinking, our relationships, and our lives. Images, and labels, are the causes of our problems, for they divide people in every relationship. And these images keep us stuck. So our perceptions of ourselves, people and life, instead of flowing as freely as a river, are dammed up, stopped by the stones of concepts and prejudices already established in the mind. This is common to all humanity.

The mind does two things, really. It thinks (storing thoughts and information, recording experiences, creating memories and images)—and it observes, looks afresh.

Thought is the past, necessary to remember your name and how to drive a car. But thought has no place in the psychological process. The mind must be free of thought to listen to someone, to observe something. Experiment with watching and listening, and don't let previous concepts interfere with perception. You don't have to think all the time. The watching, without always having opinions, is what releases you from slavery to the past. It is the really seeing something in yourself and your reactions that is the factor of change, not having some idea about what you're supposed to change into.

There was a good example of the difference between idea (previous knowledge) and insight (immediate seeing) in a sixteen-year-old girl who came to talk to me. She had been stealing from shops, a watch or a hat or a scarf. Each time she stole something, either she got into trouble or she punished herself with guilt. As we talked, we came to understand that she felt little love from the mother she needed so much. Even though she knew stealing was wrong, she stole to replace her mother's love. This understanding became knowledge. Her insight was that nothing could replace the love she needed. She stopped stealing.

So even if no one sits you down somewhere at the dinner table or a school desk and tells you how simple it is (not easy, but simple) to understand yourself by watching yourself, here are the factors:

1. there is no path or person, or ideology to follow to the truth about psychological freedom

2. truth can only be known from moment to moment, in silence, when thought is quiet, in the gaps between the noisy chatter — just listen in that silence to what you hear! — there is no time, then, only eternity in those gaps when you're not thinking, and you can hear the intelligence of the universe communicate with you

3. when you stop doing all the wrong things, only the right way will be left

If you don't believe this, try it — go sit in a corner, bring a question or problem into your mind, don't answer it or think about it —JUST LISTEN! Intelligence doesn't belong to anybody. If you can set aside your noisy selves and all those thoughts, it will come to you, too.

Try something else. Look up at the night universe and think of the forces that shaped it, that shaped earth, that produced you. You are part of that. Your subatomic matter may alter, but it will never disappear. You are part of the universe. Don't hide your face in so personal a corner or live your life in so small a box that you miss the whole glorious show.

*Section Seven*

# CULTURE, GROUPS, AND SEX

# Where Do You Come From?

It is true that early childhood trauma and your relation ships with your parents can affect your behavior for the rest of your life.

But unless they leave you in the nursery to forever thrash around in the molten lava of your own energy, several billion other forces are going to affect your behavior, too, as we have already suggested. Your peer group (people your own age you're supposed to make friends with — get along with, anyway), your sex (not your own fault), and your culture (racial, national, religious, and all that) are all going to influence you. Eventually, so will the world at large. And if you can't learn to cope with it and the people in it, they'll lock you up somewhere in some bin.

**The Meeting**

David had called a meeting in the eleventh-grade homeroom to discuss volunteer work and fund-raising for the coming school year. David was head of the Social Service Board, and he was entitled to make certain decisions himself. There were many reasons David didn't want to make the decisions alone. That was why he had called the meeting. We will examine the responses of David's group, not in terms of each individual's inner conflicts, but in terms of peer, sex, and cultural influence.

There are four on David's committee, picked for their differences in order to contribute insight into various causes: Steve, who is African American; Laurel to have a girl; Edward, WASP and wealthy; Armando, Hispanic American. David himself is Jewish.

DAVID:     *(giving each a personal glance)* I called you guys together because frankly I don't want to make all the decisions myself about where we donate our time and money. *(Because David is Jewish in a mostly gentile school, he obeys the cultural rules his parents taught him: Look, this is a gentile world. When Jews stand out too much, they get punished. If you want your way, get it persuasively, not aggressively, or they'll call you pushy. These and a lot of other rules for Jewish behavior, according to David's parents, were fed to David with his first milk. David is not only part of a religious/ethnic culture, he is also by national culture an American. Americans are theoretically influenced by the democratic principles of behavior: we vote, no one at the top just gives orders. There is also David's personal ax to grind — he would like to be the first Jewish president of the school next year and now wants group support.)*

STEVE: (nervous hand gestures) I think we ought to spread out more than we did last year. You know, instead of giving and doing for two or three organizations...(*Steve often lets his thoughts hang. Being black in a mostly white school makes him hesitant. Like David, Steve has been taught not to be too aggressive in a world where he is a member of a struggling minority. But underneath, Steve is more hostile than David. David did not grow up during World War II when Jews were under the hammer. Right now in the United States, David does not have to witness the constant put-downs of the Jews the way Steve does of African Americans. Steve has been taught to be persuasive rather than aggressive, too, but since he is an-grier, he has to keep an even tighter control on his behavior.)*

EDWARD: *(tolerant stare)* Steve, we all know what you mean. Why don't you just say it? That you want to give some of our time and money to black organizations or the African-American Scholarship Fund. I happen to agree with you. I think we should, too. And to the Hispanic groups. And the American Indian funds. All of them. *(Edward can afford to be generous. He is not only WASP and wealthy, but he comes from a Germanic-authoritarian background. His father bullies him, but he does so in the name of teaching Edward that a boy of his background is better than everyone else. As Edward looks around the room, he sees a girl, a black, a Jew, a Puerto Rican, not just four other people. He has been taught to think that way. Edward cringes under authority, but it is easy for him to feel superior to these four. Since nothing is at stake for him personally here, he can relax, without the need to bully as he has been bullied.)*

STEVE: *(with a quick look at Armando's flashing eyes)* Thanks. (It's all he can choke out. He's glad of the support, but he wished it felt less like the master patting the dogs on the head. He knows Armando is too furious to speak — as usual.)

LAUREL: I agree with Steve, too. I think we could do more things. If we had a bigger variety of choices for service, maybe more people would volunteer to work with us. David has made out a really good list. *(Smiles at David and crosses her legs, stretching a little in Edward's direction.)* Only he left out the Volunteer's Dance at the end. *(Laurel's genetic background is so mixed she can only be called plain American, but being a plain American girl these days is a rough row to hoe. One of the most important American cultural influences, because we are more success-oriented than most countries, is the personal success demanded of each child — as reflected glory on the parents. The problem for girls is that the rules have changed because of the widespread movement in the second half of the twentieth century toward gender equality for women. Before, all a girl had to do was look adorable, catch a man, get married, and have children. Now it's more complicated. Not only do girls still, according to a lot of society, have to do all that, but they have to be independent, have a career, use their brains, too. Laurel gets absolutely ex-*

*hausted from majoring in physics so she can use her brains, hiding her brains so she can please a boy, fighting off boys so she can be a "good" girl, flirting with boys so she can have a date, balancing not taking easily available drugs so she can study without risking social rejection, maintaining emotional independence so she can be her own person, yet trying to share her emotions so she can have a relationship. Trying to be a success on all fronts makes her wobbly in group discussions. She has been taught by her chauvinist father that honey gets the man, by her mother to maintain her own integrity, say what she thinks, and not worry too much about what the boys think of her. So what Laurel does is try to play it both ways. She speaks with her mind and plays footsie with her body.)*

DAVID: I left the dance out because we didn't really make that much money out of it last year and it took a lot of effort. I thought we would be better off with a raffle, getting some really good prizes by canvasing all the parents. Of course, if all of you think we ought to do the dance again, say so. Edward? *(David knows, as Steve does, that you can get Edward's support if you appeal to him first as if he had authority.)*

EDWARD:  *(He stretches his legs nearer Laurel's. He has heard David's appeal, he feels Laurel's appeal. What does Steve think? Edward must decide where to grant his favor.)* How about the dance, Steve? You helped run it last year. What do you think?

*Steve pauses. He wants Edward's support whether it kills him to angle for it or not. He knows Edward wants the dance because Edward wants to take Laurel, and Edward likes parties anyway. David doesn't want the dance, so Steve's veto could deadlock the issue, unless Armando put in a rare vote. Steve hates school dances, because they emphasize the black-white problem socially. School integration has eased some — in their school, anyway — but social integration is something else. Dances are hard on black girls. White girls think it's fun, even exotic, to dance with or date black boys. Some black boys who aren't militant about their color think it's an ego kick to have a white girl. But white boys, until they are older, don't seem to notice how beautiful black girls are, so between white and black boys, they ignore black girls at school social functions. Steve hates this, but if he doesn't go along with Edward's wishes, he will lose Edward's support to donate money or*

> *time to black causes. Steve can chance David's opposition. David will take such opposition less personally.*

STEVE:     Even if we didn't make much money, David, everyone had a pretty good time doing the dance last year. I think it gets us support for the rest of the things we do. *(Steve makes the trade. A few hours of social discomfort for a few African Americans to earn time/money/support for the African American Scholarship Fund.)*

EDWARD:     That makes three of us, David. Do we get the dance?

DAVID:     Armando?
    *Armando works hard for the Service Board. To this day, he withholds his opinions. Except from Steve, with whom he will share later on.*

So far three of them have won. Edward has had his sense of superiority fed by being appealed to. Steve has gotten the support he needs for his goal. Laurel can go home to tell her mother she has made a personal success (she knows she will be appointed Chair of the Dance Committee) and her father will be pleased because he thinks dances are a feminine number.

Now it's David's turn. He hands around copies of his list of service activities. It's a good list, he thinks. It covers all bases: a variety of scholarship funds that include all the school's cultural/gender backgrounds; a medical charity, an orphan-and-refugee campaign for countries at war as well as for homeless kids in the United States; an international environmental/ wildlife drive.

DAVID:      Add the dance, and tell me what you think
            of the list.

After a brief discussion, the list was accepted and heads of committees appointed. David had won, too.

A simple, even dull discussion. Just five teenagers sitting in a room quietly talking about a few hours of activity, a couple of hundred dollars, and a dance.

Only thousands of years of cultural conditioning — accomplishments, failures, suffering, riches, poverty, color, sex, religion — determined those few verbal responses and behavior reactions. David, Laurel, Steve, Armando, and Edward are not only the result of their personal psyches, but the products of their cultural heritages.

Erikson in his book *Childhood and Society* points out that tribes and nations use childhood training to turn out the kind of people their particular society needs. He says that sex roles are handed out, emotional and physical responses are taught, social behavior is instilled to create the kind of grown-ups who will best fit the system. To accomplish this, Erikson says, society exploits children, uses them for its own purposes. Because childhood is so long among humans, it leaves us with a lasting set of emotional immaturities. Because exploited children learn to be afraid, we retain those fears as adults. (Fears of punishment for not living up to what is expected.) He says, "In recent years we have come to the conclusion that a neurosis is psycho- and somatic, psycho- and social, and interpersonal."

Mind and body, individual and group combine to produce patterns of behavior.

Margaret Mead has done many studies of tribal people in the South Pacific. She points out that among such tribes there is no adolescence because there is no need for adolescence, no need for extra years for schooling and book-learning. There is simply puberty and marriage and the hunting and gathering and birth and death go on. There is no prolonged dependency. They have no twenty-three-year-old medical students still needing tuition money from their parents and the soul-anguish that can cause. And there isn't the adolescent who-am-I? problem, because their society makes it perfectly clear who they are from birth. You're-a-girl-you-cook, you're-a-boy-you-hunt kind of thing, though Mead is quick to point out she's found a couple of tribes where the women give the orders.

Erikson points out that in tribal societies, children are praised for contributing to adult life: gathering fruit, helping to build a boat, doing things necessary to the community's welfare. But in technologically advanced cultures, childhood is separated out from adulthood, which makes development more difficult. He has done studies to prove that play, especially the pleasure of mastery and playing adult, is necessary and healing to the child's spirit. But even playing is often conditioned by society. Boys play with "boy" things, girls with "girl" things, so that roles are conditioned early. In different cultures there are different games to encourage what is important to that particular culture.

And there are different traditions taught so the child will fit into its own culture.

The driven, success-oriented businessperson in the United States is no accident — because without status and money he's considered a failure.

The unliberated, virginal girls of Spain are no accident — because unless they "behave" no one will marry them.

The Jews who encourage their children to make a living with their brains are no accident, because for many thousands of years they weren't allowed to own land and were shunted from country to country. Their ability to earn a living had to be portable.

Hardworking African-American women who are heads of households are no accident — for too many generations the chains remained economic if not physical, and it was easier for the women to get work than the men.

The Nazi in Germany was no accident, nor were the suicidal Japanese pilots who gave their lives out of duty to their Emperor.

Each culture nourishes its own.

## Girls And Boys
## Are Equal Too

Another thing society does to you is sex.
The problem here is not what you are born with, but what you're supposed to do about it. And for ten or fifteen thousand years, society has arranged for the female psyche to be bent like a pretzel. It has arranged for the male psyche to carry an unfair overload. We're beginning to legislate

things better, but you can't legislate attitude and there's a lot of conditioning to be undone.

Girls went into the pretzel business (bending your psyche not to please yourself but to please a man and practically everybody else except yourself) probably not long after we came down out of the trees. There was a very simple reason for it. Muscle. Me bigger and stronger and will throw rocks at your head if you get out of line. And the line of work men decided on for the women was taking care of the babies and picking the berries. Nothing too intellectually stimulating for her, because then she might actually start to think and maybe figure that since she has been gathering her own nuts and berries and enough for her babies besides, she doesn't actually need a male to take care of her, and she can find an even better way to a food supply (like agriculture) or paint her own pictures on cave walls — and everybody, especially the men, knows what happens you let women think like this. They get uppity about wanting their own careers, and you lose a good source of cheap labor around the cave or the house or wherever.

So in order to keep girls in the house, it was necessary to brainwash them into believing that the only important thing in life was the love of a man, keeping his house, having his babies. Those were his because after she invented agriculture and more food was available so more babies lived she had to feed, she let him work the land and take the extra produce to market. So he got the money or shells or whatever and paid for everything, and with the guys in the mar-

ketplace — the women were all home in their separate kitchens not bonding at all — bonded together and invented the
laws and government to legalize men owning everything
including their women and children. Nothing was hers because she had no money. Nobody gets paid for being
somebody's wife. If he was a nice man and chose to share,
she was lucky. But she was no longer in control of her own
food gathering. She was dependent. She had to serve and
she had to please.

Anyway, if the most important thing in life is to catch a
man and make him love you enough to marry you, you get
the feeling you better bend yourself into some pretty pleas-
ing shapes and not leave any sharp angles of individualism
to cut into or otherwise threaten the male psyche. (If you
think the day of identical female/robot pretzels is past, check
out at any commuter train station the lineup of identical thin,
blond wives waiting next to identical four-wheel-drive trans-
port for their hunters to get off the New York City train.)

Boys have had it better in a lot of ways. They've had more
personal freedom (to experiment sexually, to choose careers), more money (their pay scale is still higher), more
power (men have always run the world — and never mind
Cleopatra or Queen Victoria; they had no effect on helping
the rest of the girls toward power equality), more education
to make more of their lives. The brain capacity is not more
or less according to sex. So there could have been just as
many female Michelangelos, Shakespeares, Einsteins, and
Mandelas. But it takes more than genius to make a career or

a talent blossom — it takes education and encouragement. And nobody was about to teach a girl to paint, write, study physics, or enter politics until very recently. So while boys went on learning, girls went on practicing how to be pretty and charming. While boys were taught how to grab the lion or the microscope or the world by the tail, girls were taught not to grab for anything to satisfy their own independent souls, but only to grab for dependency on a man. There must have been a lot of unfulfilled cavewomen staring at the cave walls (when they weren't inventing agriculture, which until recent studies, nobody's given women the credit for).

But.

There's a catch for the male of our species. Boys may be taught that the goodies of the world belong to them. But they are also taught something else.

How to kill themselves. At an early age, they are told not to cry, to be tough. So they kill a lot of tender feelings for themselves and toward others. They are told to be strong, and therefore find it hard to share a burden because that might betray a weakness. If they feel a little weakness, they hate themselves and hate the people who see it. They are told to be successful or they aren't real men. And they often literally die trying, either psychically, or physically (men die earlier than women, and more often than women, of heart attacks). They break their hearts trying because nobody lets them be human beings. They have to go on being "men" till it kills them. It can be lonely being a man. So much has to be kept hidden so the fear doesn't show. They must carry so much "responsibility" for providing for their families they've been taught they can't share.

Share is the operative word, naturally. Many women work now (women represented 46% of the civilian labor force in 1995, according to the U.S. Department of Labor), so girls could share in the working/providing (and get equal pay, of course,), and the boys could share in the nurturing (and get equal tenderness, of course), and then maybe the noise between the sexes — and maybe a lot of other noises in the world — might quiet down. (Surely it occurs to you again that men and women fighting spills into family fighting spills into neighbors fighting spills into communities fighting spills into nations fighting and everything affects everything, as we keep saying.)

Of course, the women's Second Wave movement and now the Third Wave movement of the nineties and the men's backlash and the women's backlash to the men's backlash will affect legal action. But as we've said, you can't legislate attitude. So until the day dawns when sex becomes biological instead of sociological, the psychological differences between being born a female or a male will continue to influence behavior and make it hard sometimes for boy to understand girl, and girl to understand boy.

R oger and Cindy, both sixteen, are walking down the hall. School is over for the day, and it's Friday besides. Roger has spent a lot of time thinking about Cindy. Cindy has spent a lot of time thinking about Roger. The problem is how to get the act to-

*gether. Roger has so far been very shy about girls, but he remembers something his father once said about his own first date.*

ROGER: *(feeling silly)* That backpack looks pretty heavy, Cindy. Let me carry it home for you.

CINDY: *(stunned and touched by the old-fashioned courtesy)* Thank you, Roger, I'd like that.

*When they get to the end of the hall, there is Roger, still trying to do the male thing his father taught him. Struggling with two armloads of books in backpacks, he's going to get that door open for Cindy besides. Cindy isn't sure how to react. Double over with the giggles, battle Roger for the door to equalize the situation, or let Roger pursue his male-role thing to the finish.*

*Later. Roger has asked Cindy to go out with him that evening. She has accepted.*

ROGER: What would you like to do, Cindy? *(Roger's father has told him to be nice about things like that because males are bigger and stronger and smarter and can afford to give in on small stuff that doesn't really matter.)*

CINDY: How about a movie? *(She mentions the dollar movie in the neighborhood because she knows Roger doesn't get much of an allowance and he's saving the money he makes from his part-time job for college. Cindy, herself, happens to have a twenty in her pocketbook, but heaven forbid she should take the lead — emotionally, sexually, or financially — from a boy. She wonders whether Roger would let her treat them both to coffee after the movie.)*

*Afterward. They are sitting in the dark on the back porch of Cindy's house. They have just kissed each other, and it felt very good. But neither one of them can just leave it at that. Each has a couple of points to prove.*

*Right away, after the kiss, Roger starts talking about his job, college, his future plans in civil engineering. He has been brought up to believe success is more important than love stuff except for maybe just some sex along the way. The kink is that like all human beings, Roger needs tenderness too,. He doesn't just want to make Cindy, he wants to hold her hand, be stroked, too.*

*Only that's unmanly. What's manly is to just want sex from a girl and success from the world. Besides, what would a girl think of you if she discovered that weakness known as "needing love?"*

*When, instead of reacting to their kiss, Roger starts in on how to build bigger and better sewage pipes, Cindy's sensitivities are devastated. She too has career plans, but she has been programmed to feel that love is just as important if not more important than anything else. But she can't say that to Roger because her mother has told her never to make the first move. If she kisses Roger again just to shut his mouth and get his mind back on what's going on between them, he might think she is fast and get the wrong idea about how she feels about sex. How she feels about sex is that her urge is just as strong as any boy's, but no one is supposed to know*

*that. Cindy's major feeling is why can't they fall in love and think
about careers both at the same time?*

*So they sit there. Roger feels threatened by that look of budding
love in Cindy's eyes — because he wants it and isn't supposed to
have it. Cindy feels threatened because if she falls in love with a
person like Roger, it is going to take a lot of time and energy and
might not leave time for thinking about her own medical career.*

*Cindy sighs and reaches for Roger. She has been taught too
well. Roger comes first.*

*Roger has a problem, too. As wonderful as Cindy feels in his
arms, he has been taught football —and career— come first.*

When it comes to courtesies, sex-role playing can be
fun. There is nothing wrong and a lot right and fun
about males opening doors and females rinsing a pair of
socks. But when role-playing interferes with human needs
— the female need to achieve as well as love, the male need
for love as well as achievement — it's SAD. And it's the cause
of so many misunderstandings and so much agonizing.

A few thousand years ago, it may have been necessary
for the survival of the human race that roles be divided in
physical terms. Women had the babies; male muscle de-
fended the tribe. (Of course, in some tribal peoples men
minded the babies. And I can't figure out why women
couldn't have thrown a few rocks at the enemy as well as
the men.) Anyway, that's the way we're told they did it then.
But now, since any sex can figure out a diaper and we use
machines instead of muscle, there just isn't any need to make

everybody go on pretending there's all that big a difference between male and female talents. The few inborn differences there seem to be — girls are generally born with better language and perception skills, boys are generally born with better space-relation and math skills — can be adjusted easily with educational attention.

It's better than it used to be. But behaviorally, sex can still be quite a trap no matter which one you were born. When you get awfully frustrated communicating with someone of the opposite build, try to remember the other's programming and try even harder to behave like a human instead of a sex.

# What Is Horton Wearing?

A nd don't think it doesn't matter.
Zebras know each other by their stripes.

Your parents have spent a lot of time stamping your brain with what their parents and experience have taught them are proper social responses. Always wear a tie and jacket to a job interview even if it's a road gang — to prove you come from a nice family. Or always eat in shirtsleeves even at a dinner dance to prove you don't care what anybody thinks.

Be aggressive in a group so everyone knows you have a mind of your own. Never be aggressive in a group so nobody knows if you have a mind or not. Never touch grass, or a person of the opposite sex, it's against the law (governmental, parental, Biblical). Touch it all kid, it's the only way you'll ever learn, but don't get into trouble (translation: don't get your parents into trouble).

But parental pressure isn't all you have to deal with.

*A mother, whose idea of what her young teenage daughter should wear to a party is a new skirt, was unsettled by her daughter's insistence, on being invited to her first home party, that everybody in her group wore jeans only, everywhere. The mother did her psychic best, according to her own lights, by buying her daughter a good-looking shirt and a brand new pair of jeans. At least the kid would look neat and put together. What the kid did was come home to say she wished she'd had a heart attack instead. What everybody else was wearing were ratty patches, not — I wish I were dead — new clothes!*

Peer group pressure, it's called, and it's not always as easy to deal with as getting the kind of clothes your friends are wearing. Although there's a point to clothes. It's the way they make you feel about yourself. It's looking as if you belong even if you don't always feel as if you do belong. It's bad enough being pushed around by the inner torture of "am I acceptable?" without having to worry about standing out like a sore thumb in your clothes besides.

Peer group pressure to conform, pressure from people your own age who want you to behave the way they do so that everyone feels solid — happens all your life. People feel threatened by those who behave and dress and talk differently. But it's especially difficult to cope with peer pressure during your teens. Your basic drives and inner parental voices are much stronger than your sense of your own reality, so it's much harder for you to make reality-based decisions — what do I really want, what is really good for the person that is me. Obviously you can't surrender to every parental command, or you'll never be independent. Obviously you can't surrender to your basic drives all the time, or you'll be a wreck or in jail. So your unnerved sense of reality checks on what your group is doing, for support for its own behavior. The weaker and more dependent you are, the more you will conform to group pressures to earn the support and approval of at least somebody, even if not your own or your parents. The stronger you are, the more decisions you will be able to make based on what is right for you as a person. (This does not mean sticking out like a sore thumb in public just to prove a point: consideration for others, a touch of modesty, and the threat of expulsion forbid wearing a bikini and chains to school.)

We human beings are social animals. We travel in herds, not alone. Everybody is part of some kind of group: school, family, job, friends, something. You can risk your neck by climbing out on a limb, or melt so safely into the pack no one will ever notice you again — or, like most of us, race back and forth from limb to pack in one way or another. But always, whatever you do, your peers, because of their needs to prove their own norms are correct, will make you feel pressure. You want to wear your jeans backward? Go right ahead, but watch it! Your bunch may go whoopee and zip up backward, too (which makes you group leader), or you could end up earning a name for yourself you might or might not like.

The big norms (standards of behavior) your peer group really aims to control are sex, drugs, alcohol, doing school work well or not, and deciding on accepted activities from gangs, guns, and crime to teaching Sunday school.

There are schools, and not just in inner cities, where the pressure to have sex, carry guns, use and deal drugs, get drunk, be part of certain groups — even if they are not called gangs — for the purposes of theft, arson, and general mayhem, makes it hell for the kid who just wants to get through school and learn something. Some city schools are like high-security prisons, with gun checks. (There were 135,000 guns brought into schools in one 1997 television report.) No gang colors are allowed, ID cards must be carried to keep intruders out, only plastic and styrofoam can be used in cafeterias. No doors are allowed in washrooms to provide hideouts. Security systems include hall cameras, locking-in of the students after school opens, no loitering in halls.

And this is nothing to the imprisonment of children in projects, in ghettos, who live at home behind barred doors and windows in an attempt at safety, who can't go out to play in the violent streets, who not only have few role models, but even in their own hallways encounter an older generation lost to hope, the dealers using teenagers to carry drugs and do the shooting. There is the impact of a war zone on these kids. At least in Bosnia, children think the war will end. Not here. And here it's not even clear who the enemy is for kids.

Even kids who live in small, quiet towns or on the Park Avenues of bigger cities know they live under most of the same threats.

Start with a party in any average American home. Everybody else at the party (whether they secretly want to or not) is smoking grass and making out. Your inner parental voices (even if your parents discuss their own drug use and whether they continue to use or not) give you a definite no-no. Your deeper basic drives of wanting comfort, curiosity, holler yummy. Your peer group is giving you an okay on the scene. What reality-based decision in terms of what's good for you, what you feel about it, are you going to come up with? If you don't get into the act, maybe your peers will think you're weird and that's the end of your social life. If you do what they're doing without feeling okay about it, you may hate yourself in the morning. You know perfectly well your girl friend in the corner is making out with a boy she doesn't like just to be part of the group. Can you do that? You also know that boy in the corner gets sick on the dope he's smoking along with the coke he's already had. Besides, good or bad, it's all still not legal. There are some very high people at the party who carry guns. A neighbor's call to the police could get serious.

Maybe you'll decide to just stop thinking about it all so much. You'll decide to stay away from the marijuana, and just join in the making out because a boy you like anyway is smiling at you. You might wish you really could go out with him first, talk, get to know him before you wrap around him. Still, you think it will feel good, and besides, everybody else in the world is doing it! Being left out of the party everyone here, everyone you see on television, seems to be having, is too scary. You want to be part of the group action.

A lot of people say, "If it feels good, do it."

Feels good to what? Just your body? What about your psyche? And will it feel good tomorrow or just this minute? And while everybody needs friends, are these exactly the friends you need? How does all this fit into your view of yourself? Or if you're temporarily experimenting with different roles and images, how far out can you go and still get back?

Since we're dealing with the psyche, not final answers, a more objective measure of your own behavior versus group pressure might be, "If you can handle it, do it."

But be careful of the word handle.

Nobody's psyche can really handle the public humiliation of a drug charge.

Nobody's psyche can handle too much parental disapproval.

Nobody's psyche can really handle sex until she or he is emotionally mature enough to be responsible to and for another human being (never mind the possibilities of pregnancy, STD's, AIDS). No matter how people, boys as well as girls, repress their feelings — feelings, not just bodies, happen during sex, and someone can and usually does get hurt.

If you think through whether you can handle something emotionally before you act out, you'll have developed a pretty good psychic defense, both against your own needs and the pressures of your group. Every time you betray yourself by doing something under pressure you don't feel right about, you get weaker. And right now, you need all the help from yourself you can get! Don't suddenly go stupid and dump on yourself.

Take a look at what Horton is wearing, but also think whether his yellow, high-heeled boots would look exactly terrific on you.

But more important, take a look at what Horton is doing. Do you really want ten girl friends, a Harley, a string of arrests, a destroyed brain, an unlimited allowance, and already-made partnership in a multimillion-dollar business — with a father who attaches iron strings to every goody? If you can handle it, try. Start with the boots.

*Section Eight*

# MENTAL
# ILLNESS

# Who's A Nut?

We all are. Just to be human is upsetting.

It's only a matter of degree as to how upset you get.

As you read this section, you won't be able to help looking for signs of mental illness in yourself, for symptoms or patterns of behavior beyond the "normal" range. Guess what. You'll find them. One of them, some of them, all of them.

The reason for that is that we all exhibit "abnormal" patterns of behavior sometimes. The person who is shy and withdrawn at a party is exhibiting the same form of behavior as the schizophrenic patient curled up against a hospital wall. The difference is that reasonably healthy people bounce back from stress, do not lose touch entirely with reality, and go on with their lives. It's mostly a matter of degree.

The simplest definition of a mentally healthy person is one whose psyche can cope with internal and external reality well enough to get the person through life without suffering so much he or she can't function. Or causing so much suffering that other people can't function. If you harm yourself so you can't cope, or you harm others, help is necessary. Your psyche has to be reasonably enough well-organized so that you can behave in a socially acceptable manner. Mastery, most of the time, over internal and external stress is the general meaning of mental health.

That doesn't mean you can't have fits once in a while or depressions or even experience the whole range of emotional and behavioral patterns from murder in your heart to times of quiet withdrawal. But if you're still managing to get through your classes and wash your face and nobody's dead on the floor, including your own soul, for any length of time, you're probably okay.

Nobody knows enough yet about the mind to know just how much suffering is enough or too much. Or to make hard and fast definitions about mental illness. There are, of course, behavior patterns that make society tend to lock up some of its members. Criminals, the psychotic, those with severe retardation, people who behave too strangely make the rest of us nervous, so we put them in prisons and asylums. We put them away partly for our own sense of physical safety and theirs. But we also put them away because we identify with them to some degree. They make us uncomfortable because they are a threat to our own stability. Seeing them, we fear our own loss of control. It isn't always easy to stay "sane." We don't want any reminders around us of damaged minds.

## A Matter of Degree
## and Types of Behavior

There are people who seem to be ordinary, yet cause a lot of pain to others and to themselves. There are people who do not take their clothes off in public, rob banks, push heroin, drive drunk, or create disturbances of any public kind. Some are so isolated and alone, they face one long, gray day after another, totally cut off from all human relationships. These people aren't bothering anybody, but they aren't functioning well either. There are people who are unkind, indifferent to their children, verbally cruel to other people, snub, disrespect, hate. Psychically, they are just as sick as some of those we lock away. Mental illness can't be defined by who is or isn't put in a straight jacket.

Who is suffering? Who is or is not functioning? Who lives only in fantasy? Who is or isn't coping well with the realities of life, the pain, the joy, the difficulties? Who is abnormal, normal? Who doesn't need help and who does, and what kind? Since no two people reflect the human condition identically, how do you arrive at a satisfactory definition of what anyone could or should be?

Words are not the same as feelings or states of mind, but since we can't always touch and sense one another, words are what we've got to at least try to define what is going on inside all of us. Labels can't describe or help a whole human being. But we need them as a sort of general shorthand to describe general states of being.

## Mental Illness

A lot of psychiatrists, psychologists, social workers, neuroscientists, and others in the mental health field protest each other's definitions about even using that term. They sometimes simply say "personality maladjustment" — which doesn't help much either. It just means a person can't manage — which may be as good a definition as any. The brain is unable to respond or adapt accurately to the real world.

Mental illness is not fun — ever, says Hannah Carlson in her book *I Have A Friend with Mental Illness*. To someone who has a mental illness, life can sometimes be a nightmare, often terrifying and bizarre, always a prison of isolation. Mental illnesses involve disorders of thinking, feeling, judgment, and behavior. Diagnoses identify a person's distressed feelings; obsessive, irrational, and/or psychotic thoughts; compulsive, disruptive, socially unacceptable, possibly dangerous behaviors. The degree of any of these is what determines whether or not someone needs hospitalization or out-patient treatment. Mental illness should be thought of and respected, diagnosed and treated, as a legitimate illness.

Mental illnesses, like other illnesses, are diagnosed by their symptoms. The Diagnostic Statistical Manual—IV (DSM-IV) is the recognized manual psychiatrists and psychologists use to diagnose mental illnesses. Some of the most common mental illnesses are grouped into:

- schizophrenia and other psychotic disorders

- mood disorders

- personality disorders

- anxiety disorders

- dissociative disorders

## SCHIZOPHRENIA AND OTHER PSYCHOTIC DISORDERS

The word psychotic is generally used for disturbances that include a loss of contact with reality and the experience of hallucinations and delusions. Schizophrenia can be described as not being able to tell the difference between what people are experiencing and what is really happening to them. They seem unable to understand the reality of situations and are unable to relate effectively to people or to work. They may have delusions (imagine scars, for instance, where there are none). They may have hallucinations (most often auditory) and hear voices, perhaps commanding them to behave in certain ways. Hallucinations can involve any of the other senses as well, sight, touch, taste, and smell. Often the hal-lucinations are frightening, threatening, even brutally criti-cal. There may be delusional schizophrenia, as in someone trying to poison them, or someone madly in love with them. There may be paranoid schizophrenia, of elaborate plots of persecution, comparing themselves to or believing them-selves to be Joan of Arc, Gandhi, god.

## MOOD DISORDERS

**Major Depression.** There is a drop in mood, a loss of in-terest and pleasure in life, a gain or loss of appetite, gain or loss of a lot of weight, sleep problems, concentration prob-lems, feelings so sad or bad there are thoughts of suicide. It's like living underwater or in a dark hole they can't climb out of, without energy, without light. This can last days, weeks, months, even years at a time.

**Manic Depression.** The same feelings of depression as above alternate with highs so giddy, people with this disor-der will have the energy of ten, little need to sleep, be hy-peractive, unrestrained, impulsive, and do everything to excess: they will talk too much, too fast; spend too much money too fast; take risks of all kinds and get into trouble, injure themselves, end up in jails and hospitals.

## PERSONALITY DISORDERS

These disorders are characterized by a life time of con-flict and distress. The pain is the faulty perception of the self and relationships with others.

**Borderline Personality.** People with this disturbance will go to any extreme to avoid real or imagined abandonment. They seesaw between criticizing themselves and inflating their self-importance. Their relationships with others are equally unstable, one minute desperately needy, the next, rejecting. They have few inner resources, they may hurt themselves physically (self-mutilation), threaten or try suicide. They are reactive and impulsive, and with little self-insight, may have little ability to relate to the very other people they need so much.

**Obsessive-Compulsive Personality.** They are preoccupied by senseless thoughts or routines that intrude into daily activities. Their repetitive thoughts and routines interrupt their lives and can drive their friends and families up a tree. Repeated hand-washing, checking and rechecking to make sure doors are locked, stoves and lights are turned off, rugs are straight, lists are completed, in a ritualized and repetitious manner, are external manifestations. They may be forced to think distressing thoughts, repeat fantasies over and over again, as well as behaviors. Addiction, drugs, alcohol, shopping, gambling are all forms of obsessive-compulsive behavior. These routines and thought patterns can become so overwhelming that they consume most or all of the day and interfere with jobs, family and social life, isolating the person with this disorder in his or her own distress.

**Anxiety Disorders.** They cannot control worries or concerns. Distressing thoughts consume attention and energy. They worry about their well-being, the outcome of situa-

tions, the well-being of self or others until their chronic worrying exhausts them and everybody else. We all experience
anxiety sometimes, even during certain stress periods,
deeply. For those who suffer from an anxiety disorder, the
feeling is always present.

**Agoraphobia.** Worries of safety in open places often prevent people who suffer this disorder from even leaving the
house. So frightened of being caught someplace dangerous
where they can't escape without difficulty or embarrassment,
they experience panic attacks (heart racing, difficulty with
breathing, sweats). This fear can imprison people in their
own rooms.

There are many other kinds of phobias, or fears. There is
fear of height, darkness, closed spaces, among them.

**Post Traumatic Stress Disorder.** People who have experienced or witnessed an event where there was actual or
threatened death, or serious injury or violence and whose
reaction to this was extreme helplessness, fear, or horror,
suffer from this. They will go on re-experiencing the event
or events in dreams, memory, or in a sense distress like a
loud noise. PTSD is frequently found among children and
adults who have experienced abuse, war, terrorist acts, do-
mestic violence, rape, and other violent crimes.

## DISSOCIATIVE DISORDERS

**Dissociative Amnesia**. After a traumatic or intensely
stressful event, people may defend their minds from the
painful memory by forgetting who they are or any other
personal information. The forgetting may be so complete,

even loved ones are not recognized. People who live with this illness live in frightening confusion. They feel unconnected to their own lives.

**Dissociative Identity Disorder.** Formerly known as multiple personality disorder, this manifests itself as two or more personalities or identities that take control of the behavior of one person. It seems that people who have suffered severe physical or sexual abuse as children suffer this disorder most often. It has been suggested that the number of personalities may reflect the number of abuses. Often the personalities do not know of each other. Often one personality may endanger the others or other people. The point of new personality invention to begin with was to escape the trauma experienced by the original personality.

CAUSES

Specific causes of mental illness, such as particular genes, structures, or chemicals in the brain, or social and environmental influences, have been the subject of much research and controversy. Many scientists, psychologists, psychiatrists, and social workers agree that the causes of mental illness involve a combination of physiological, neurochemical, psychological, and social factors.

**Drugs and Disease**

*Drugs.* Alcohol, LSD, dexedrine, and other drugs make people behave like psychotics, but for chemical not psychological reasons. These drugs can have long-lasting and serious effects.

*Diseases.* Psychoses (clinical disorders), mood disorders, personality disorders, anxiety disorders, all of these can result from certain diseases such as multiple sclerosis, stroke, long-term syphilis, Altzheimer's disease.

Brain degeneration from old age, destruction of brain tissue from injury, changes in the oxygen content in the blood, high fevers, medications for other diseases — all these things may cause psychotic reaction. Many, though not all, physical psychoses can be corrected or else the symptoms can be lessened by proper medications.

## Brain Chemistry

Because of the sophisticated level of pharmacology, chemistry, molecular biology, and imaging technology, all disciplines that study brain activity, researchers have been able to demonstrate chemical and biological connections to and possible physical causes for mental illness. For example people with mental illness are likely to have one or more other family members with mental illness. Specific nerve cells in the brain have been connected to the existence of and cure for mental illnesses. This suggests a genetically impaired condition that may be inherited.

For instance, consider the sociopath or psychopath, the one without a conscience who feels nothing akin to compassion or even sympathy and can kill, torture, mutilate without a shred of remorse. Scientists are beginning to discover genetic/chemical factors in their DNA, their brain scans, that differ from the norm.

We all know about drugs like Ritalin that seem to help kids with ADHD, attention-deficit-hyperactivity disorder. (Do always investigate both need and side effects before considering the use of this or any drug. Get second, third, and fourth opinions, especially where you, teenagers, or younger children are concerned.)

New chemicals seem to help those with schizophrenia, supplying what is missing or needed to reconnect them with reality. New drugs seem to help depression. Nerve cell chemicals such as dopamine and serotonin have been identified with mental illnesses such as schizophrenia, obsessive-disorder, and depression. When there is either too much or too little of certain chemicals in the brain, researchers have found the results may show as mental disorders. When a chemical balance is obtained through medication, the mental disorders have been seen to significantly improve or disappear.

**Pregnancy and Birth**

Prenatal influences such as the mother using drugs (nicotine is also a drug) or alcohol (also a drug), contracting influenza or suffering severe malnutrition increase the likelihood of the baby developing mental illness. Labor and delivery complications (oxygen deprivation, abnormal delivery, infections), may also increase the likelihood of a baby developing mental illness.

### Other Medical Disorders

Psychotic symptoms have been linked with other medical disorders, such as brain tumors, temporal lobe epilepsy, multiple sclerosis, sarcoidosis, Huntington's disease, cerebral vascular accidents (strokes), and AIDS, to name a few.

### Environmental Causes

Social, cultural, and environmental components of mental illness, such as neglect, abuse, and traumatic experiences, have always been known to increase mental illness, especially when the abuse or the witnessing of abuse happens in childhood. This has been documented in cases of second generation Holocaust survivors, American slavery and prejudice victims, Vietnam war veterans, victims of incest and physical abuse, victims of homelessness and poverty and crime.

## SURVIVE OR THRIVE

Many people diagnosed with mental illnesses show significant improvement with the right therapies and treatments, with support and understanding at home, school, at work, in the community. But the medications and the care are only part of the solution.

We could do something even more helpful. We could, as we are doing in this book, examine our attitudes about ourselves, our values, about war, crime, prejudice, and the way the human race has been thrashing about for a million or more years. We can decide whether we are just to survive — or actually thrive together.

# Addiction

**Alcoholism**

Alcoholism is not the same as heavy drinking, although heavy drinking may be a sign of future alcoholism. There are sweet little old ladies who are alcoholics on two glasses of sherry a day, and businessmen entertaining clients who swallow quarts who are not alcoholics. The difference between alcoholics and just drinkers is the dependency, physical and mental, on liquor, and the effect, what alcohol does to the personality. And alcoholism is progressive. It gets worse. The sweet little old lady may only drink two glasses of sherry, but she needs that sherry desperately, thinks about it, looks forward to it, and is full of anxiety if something interrupts her drinking pattern. The businessman who may down a quart a day for weeks can go off happily on a white-water raft without a bottle. In other words, he can stop whenever he likes. The alcoholic cannot stop the craving. The alcoholic also cannot depend on behavior once the drink is inside. On two glasses of sherry, the sweet little old lady might turn into a tootsie-of-the-evening. On a quart of whiskey, the not-alcoholic businessman will simply pass out. Also, the sweet little old lady will probably have blackouts. She will behave as if she's conscious of what she's doing, but not remember a thing in the morning. Non-alcoholics will pass out. Alcoholics may pass out, too. But only alcoholics will have blackouts. Unlike the businessman who can stop whenever he likes, the alcoholic's obsession with alcohol never stops. The drinking can be given up for short periods of time, but without help, insight, a program to help, the obsession goes on for the rest of the alcoholic's life.

Alcoholism, as opposed to normal drinking, is a disease. It is, scientists find today, a biochemical imbalance, probably inherited. Certainly, drinking enough to find out you are an alcoholic is a regressive behavior. But whether it is a chemical or mental disease or both, it is, so far, incurable. Once an alcoholic, always an alcoholic, whether a drinking one or a sober one. If the alcoholic drinker doesn't give up alcohol, the active disease becomes progressive. More and more waking hours are spent drunk. The ability to face anything without a drink is lost, as are jobs, families, human relationships, everything. Physically, the body begins to show symptoms. The liver may become enlarged and diseased. There may be malnutrition because serious drinkers drink and do not eat. Worst of all there may be permanent brain damage, because booze destroys brain cells permanently.

The well-dressed, underage, alcoholic sixteen-year-old girl, rich enough to sit in a bar and drink, and the homeless, evil-smelling Bowery bum have more in common with each other than either does with the rest of the world. They care more about the bottle than anything else, and unless helped, will end up seriously damaging their chances of survival. Little green bugs and large pink elephants are at the end of both of their lines. Or jail. Or a horrible death.

Most psychiatrists who treat patients who are also alcoholics have discovered that therapy doesn't help the alcoholic problem as much as Alcoholics Anonymous, a fellowship of teenagers and adults, men and women, who have a desire to stop drinking and stay stopped, who meet in groups all over the world, often in church basements or school auditoriums, to help each other stop drinking. AA is accessible, leaderless, free. If you have it, a dollar coffee-and-cookie contribution gets you thousands of dollars of the most appropriate help just for the asking. Their success record has been much higher than other forms of therapy, mostly because alcoholics understand their own problems, con games, slips from sobriety, better than nonalcoholics — and they stay sober by helping each other.

Alcoholics may be daily drinkers, weekend drinkers, a bout here and there binge drinkers. It's not the amount or the when that counts, it's the dependency, the addiction, the inability to comfortably stop drinking when one should, the progression, and the personality changes that cause trouble during the drinking.

## Drug Addiction

It seems a lot more people can take a drink without becoming an alcoholic than can take other drugs without becoming an addict. Even if you're not hung up psychologically, taking drugs seems to create a physical dependence, a body craving that blows the mind even if the mind was going to be perfectly okay.

Not only does drug dependency hideously torture the mind and body, but it involves the users in crime, prostitution, humiliating experiences, and often prison. To feed the craving, which grows larger all the time, money — a lot of money — has to be gotten. Drugs are not legal like alcohol, and those who are hooked eventually find themselves in trouble with the law.

The pressured teenager may start with a little grass borrowed from a friend. She may do a little coke, try Ecstasy once at a rave, pop an upper, an amphetamine, a downer, a barbiturate, experiment with hashish, mushrooms, LSD, in-

halants, heroin — all just so she knows what's in. Her boyfriend might, for kicks, take some stimulants or tranquiliz-
ers or whatever from his parents' medicine cabinet — pre-
scription drugs are always available as well as street drugs.
But morphine, cocaine, heroin, LSD in some form or another
are the glamor drugs. They are also the most addictive. The
more you take, naturally, the more you need. The more you
need, the more it costs. The progression is obvious. So is the
need for money. The drugs are illegal. The ways to acquire
enough money to feed growing habits are illegal. Both involve dealing eventually in a filthy world more awful than
anything most teenagers have seen except on television. But
the withdrawal symptoms without the drugs make for an
equally horrible suffering.

The numbers of narcotic addicts in the United States is
growing. Surveys show that from 1992-1996, drug use among
12-17-year-olds more than doubled — and that there was
little difference in responses whether they lived in poor cities or rich suburbs.

The two major problems in experimenting with that first
little bit of marijuana — are: first, it's illegal (possible trouble
right there); and second, people never know until it's too
late whether they are potential addicts, and the marijuana
will lead to harder drugs.

I have worked in wards of veteran's hospitals where men
were brought off drug habits over and over again, habits
acquired in Vietnam twenty years ago and more, by the
methadone treatment, a drug used to help people get through

the painful withdrawals. Symptoms include weakness, muscular pain, vomiting, severe agitation, depression, the shakes, among others. I have seen teenagers in Phoenix House in New York City struggle with the same thing, habits more recently acquired. It's always the same. Some come from and go back to lives where there is little hope and drugs are easy to get. Often they come back again and again for treatment. Others, with better motivation and some unknown quality go off to Narcotics Anonymous or other ongoing program and move on with their lives. But all are going to spend the rest of their days, like alcoholics, being careful, watchful of their obsession for drugs.

The trouble with addiction is addiction. It never ends.

# Brain Damage

There are many ways brain tissue can be damaged, causing mental retardation, psychotic behavior, physical deformities, paralysis, spastic problems, seizures, blindness, early death.

Children with brain damage should be diagnosed as early as possible, cared for and taught as much as possible — if possible — so that whatever their life spans, they can feel as if they are part of the human race instead of frightened outcasts. Unfortunately, too much of society is still horrified or afraid of those who are mentally or physically deformed, horrified at what they have produced, afraid of what they might produce, fearful of what they might have been themselves, even that what they see in other is somehow catching.

Feeling helpless to help, hopelessly uninformed, not understanding the causes and conditions, people lock these children away in institutions, some of which are worse than animal cages. It is true that many of these children cannot be cared for at home and must live out their lives where there is medical supervision. And it is true that there are many fine institutions. But it is also true that many of these children could be cared for at home if only families, neighbors, communities could love instead of be shocked by them. And if we offered more help, so that outpatient community clinical, educational, therapeutic help were locally available in more places. There must be more day schools for those with mental retardation in all communities. Take, for example, one form of mental retardation, a most frequent one, once called mongolism, but more properly known as Down's syndrome. People with this don't always need an institution. Although their intellectual levels may be low, they are cheerful and loving, and they take eager pleasure in doing simple useful tasks and being part of community and family life. Their problem, often, is the way people react to their looks — small head, slanted eyes with a fold, poor control over certain muscles. Some families just don't want to cope, no matter how sweet-tempered the children are.

Down's syndrome is just one form of brain damage that can happen to the baby inside the womb. It is not hereditary.

In *I Have A Friend With Mental Retardation*, Hannah Carlson says, "People can be born with or acquire mental retardation in a variety of ways. Physical disorders or syndromes may accompany mental retardation…and…can cause defects in formation and function of…spine and brain development."

There are hereditary factors that can cause malformed brains, chemical imbalances, chromosomal disorders, skin and nerve disorders, muscular, craniofacial, skeletal disorders, developmental disorders of brain formation like spina bifida. There can be complications during pregnancy such as Rh factors, or drug addiction in the mother, syphilis, X-ray of pregnant uterus, drugs like thalidomide, diseases a mother contracts in the first few months of pregnancy such as German measles, malnutrition. Some of the results are absence of part of brain tissue, microcephaly (abnormally small brain and head formation), hydrocephaly (too much fluid pressing on and eventually shrinking the brain until it stops functioning, often causing early death). There are problems in and around labor and delivery, infections after birth like meningitis. There can be head injuries, accidents or abuse, infections like encephalitis, degenerative disorders like Parkinson's disease, seizure disorders, and so on.

And finally, there are the Unknown Causes. Many cases of mental retardation have as yet no identifiable cause.

Mental retardation is measured in many ways, only one of which is the familiar IQ testing. Other factors include the ability to cope with self-care, home living, communication social skills, community use, health and safety, self-direction, work. You don't always need genius IQ levels to cope with those.

Often children with low IQ's improve them with good care and love. With these, they certainly lead less miserable lives. While it is true that children with mental retardation can't always cope with the world at large, they can thrive in the protected environment of a home. Training centers and schools, clinics, and public and parent education have changed many negative attitudes, and we are learning all the time about ways to develop such abilities as these children and teenagers have.

There are still other problems, other patterns of behavior about which little is still really understood. There is the child with autism, who won't or can't relate in any meaningful way to people in the world, whose senses get so overloaded, it makes them scream to be touched or held, for whom even a pale light hurts the eye, for whom music is thunder.

There are learning disabilities. This is a processing problem that has nothing to do with mental retardation or mental illness. Often people with learning disabilities, like Einstein and Mozart and Hans Christian Andersen, are our greatest geniuses. A learning disability may mean your left brain can't process language very well, so speech and spelling are a problem. Or your right brain is impaired, so relationships to social situations can be a problem as with Einstein. Learning disabilities like dyslexia (reading dysfunctions) are nerve problems, neurological impairments. There are verbal learning disabilities and nonverbal learning disabilities, like the social skills problems mentioned, or math skills problems, or spacial-relationship problems like those in geometry or in parking a car. Children and teenagers, as well as adults, with learning disabilities often turn out to be extremely bright.

## Organic Brain Disorders

Bad things can also happen to the brain of an older person that can cause it to stop functioning well, that can create psychotic behavior patterns without psychological history for such behavior, and that force it to lose its ability to learn, understand, function, judge.

*Senility.* Just getting old, changes in the nervous systems that make the memory fail, and make it difficult to adapt to any changes. Senility may remain relatively minor, or progress to bring about a total vegetablelike existence. (Not to be confused with Alzheimer's disease.)

*Alcoholic psychosis, infections* such as syphilis, encephalitis, diseases such as cerebral arteriosclerosis, and other central nervous system diseases can destroy brain tissue and create psychotic behavior patterns.

*Strokes* can cause parts of the brain to shut down and paralyze the body.

*Head injuries* from falls or blows can cause varying amounts of brain damage.

Such organic brain disorders are either acute (they happen suddenly and there is hope for recovery) or chronic (disorders develop more slowly and progressively get worse). The treatment and care of such patients consists of trying to repair the damage as much as possible and to reeducate the patient to accept a lesser ability to function.

We have a long way to go in solving the problems of the mind, whether physically or not physically caused.

But there is some help. And more help is on the way. And if you have problems that interfere with the way you really want to live, get whatever help you can. From the novel Peter Ibbetson, by George DuMaurier: "Poor human nature, so richly endowed with nerves of anguish, so splendidly organized for pain and sorrow, is but slenderly equipped for joy."

If you're a lot short on joy, a little therapy couldn't hurt. All human brains are, to some degree, limited. We all see and hear only what our brains' receptors are conditioned to see and hear, all physics to the contrary. For instance, we see form instead of energy and light (you and I and the table under my computer are just atoms in space, not you and I and a table), and we are preoccupied with things that don't exist; for example self and psychological time (both invented by thought). Most of us have no notion that we see not what is there, but what our brains have been taught to see. And we suffer from shadows — try to hold your past or your future in the palm of your hand. Surely, these limitations are a learning disability common to us all.

Specific psychological problems are real, and in our success-through-winning oriented society, they can be frightening and isolating. But before you start hating yourself for having psychological problems or develop prejudices about someone else who has some, try to remember all human brains are still blundering about after millions of years of so-called evolution.

*Section Nine*

---

# DIALOGUE, THERAPY, THE USES OF PSYCHOLOGY

**P**ain happens. The point of psychology, the study of the mind and behavior, is to learn that you don't have to suffer so much over the pain that happens to you.

Whether it's biology or environment, it's all conditioning, and conditioning is what we are interested in getting beyond when it causes pain.

You'll discover mental pain comes from:

1.  wanting what you don't have and have been taught to want or need

2.  being afraid to lose what you do have

3. having an image of yourself someone pokes a hole in, like thinking of yourself as smart and someone calls you stupid

4. being left out, or being afraid of being left out, of life's party

At the bottom of most human mental suffering is what we call loneliness. It's a word we have been taught to use. Some call that emptiness just — peace. They know it's a gift — an empty place for the beauty of the world, for joy, to come in. (Obviously, if you've crammed this place inside you full of busyness, there's no room for *It*.) So, if you can, enjoy your inner space. If you can't enjoy it, the best therapy I know when loneliness hits, is to remember everybody's got it, so you're not alone. Not with roughly 6 billion people bumping into each other all over the same planet. Hold mental hands with all of us, and you won't be lonely any more.

Most people run, escape from the loneliness by looking for security, in other people, places, and things. Then you're back to the pains listed above. There's no security really, except to learn how to live insecurely, freely, in the world. You can get through a day or a week or longer of some psychological pain. No one remembers to tell you this, so it scares you. Just don't fix it with the wrong things, or you'll be stuck with two problems, the original suffering and a bad fix. You can't opt for both safety and freedom anyway — and since it's looking for safety that causes the pain, try freedom.

If all that's the matter with you is that you sometimes overeat to comfort yourself because you're lonely, or you collect Coke cans as a displacement for a full enough sex life, you probably aren't in terrible trouble. Everybody has a few pleasures to compensate for occasional feelings of being unloved, or of self-hate or of worthlessness. Now and then depression — especially in adolescence when the chemistry of the body is changing, states of being and attention are changing, both dependence and independence are fearsome — or anxiety-ridden elations, or the absolute knowledge that nobody ever has or will understand you, are part of the human condition. We do seem adequately wired for a great deal more suffering than joy.

Dialogue with people who are also aware of themselves helps more than anything. Insight will change your mood faster than jet skis. And don't be afraid of the unconscious stuff — it's just like the conscious stuff, only it's stuck under there like a sharp piece of glass. This can cut into you pretty well, but it's not too hard to get out if you're willing to look for it. This is all part of meditation, meaning, simply, to pay attention.

But if emotional problems haunt you to distraction. If behavior patterns as severe as addiction, inability to relate closely to anybody, to get along with friends and family at all, to manage at school in terms of marks, or to control anti-social behavior like fighting or stealing are seriously interfering with your ability to function, some kind of therapy may be necessary, along with meditation.

We're all a little crazy. It just depends on whether your particular form of craziness is derailing your entire life. Humans are predators (check out your eyes, they are in the front of your head, not on the side like those of prey).

We scare ourselves as well as everybody else. Don't get psychotic over this, get help. And for people who say, "I may be all wrong, but this is how I want to be," you can think about how many things you want (two motorcycles, the corner on happy juice, the entire floor of Filene's) that aren't necessarily good for you.

The more serious forms of mental illness, learning disabilities, developmental disabilities, and disorders due to brain damage will probably have been detected by the time you read this book. And if you can actually read this book, they have obviously either been attended to or observed by you one way or another.

For the moment, let's only be concerned with the usual problems of getting over the bad bumps, the normal abnormal crises that happen one time or another in everybody's life.

## Who Can Help

Let's go over the kinds of people who can help you with psychological problems besides friends and family.

FAMILY DOCTOR

Your knees hurt you, or you get too many headaches, or you find yourself with a compulsion to steal other people's pencil cases. You tell your mother, or some fink at school tells your mother. And the first person she calls is the family doctor. He has an M.D. degree, is supposedly a pretty good diagnostician. He may be able to advise about problems in addiction, psychosomatic symptoms, sexual difficulties, eating disorders, and so forth. If the problem seems severe, he will have enough sense to recommend the right kind of specialist. Sometimes, all that's the matter is that you hate your father or your mother or both, or any or all of your sibs, at a time when such feelings are normal, and you need a little therapy for a few months so you can get a bead on your feelings and let your anger out somewhere safe. Sometimes, of course, the problem can be more serious. You really did and are having a horrible life.

## THE PSYCHIATRIST

The psychiatrist not only has an M.D., she or he has had special training for three or more years in various problems of human behavior. The psychiatrist not only has had training in psychotherapies of various kinds, both individual and group, but training in administering drugs and the legal ability to prescribe them.

## THE PSYCHOANALYST

The psychoanalyst has had all of the above training plus five to seven years of personal psychoanalysis to help in understanding yours, although not all psychoanalysts are psychiatrists (doctors as well as analysts). Without an M.D., however, there can be no administration of drugs.

THE PSYCHOLOGIST

This is someone with a Ph.D. degree, usually requiring three to five years of study after college, but not a physician with a medical degree. The training emphasizes clinical psychology, research, diagnostic training, treatment, and testing. Psychologists work in institutions, hospitals, schools, universities, clinics, to determine the tests to be administered, the best treatment, and who could best carry out treatment. Often they practice individual and group therapies themselves.

OTHER HELP

There are also psychiatric nurses, social workers, rehabilitation workers, case workers, vocational counselors, and counselors in everything from general mental healthy to sex problems, from geriatric psychology to teenage and child psychology. There are all kinds of therapists, clinics, mental health centers, and state, private, or general hospital outpatient clinics. There are family service agencies, veteran's hospitals, community hospitals, youth centers, Planned Parenthood Centers, hotlines of all kinds especially for teenagers in trouble: runaways; pregnant teens, gay and lesbians who have problems; those with addiction problems.

In short, there is a lot of help at hand, if you can just manage to find the right kind: the kind that helps you; the kind you can afford; the kind that cares enough to follow through on your problems, diagnose your problems correctly, and place you where you can be helped, not nailed to the wall.

## What Can Help

- *Psychotherapy* (treatment of the mind) has to suit the situation. Someone I once knew had severe problems with feelings of worthlessness, failure, and self hate. He was told to join an encounter group, where a lot of people get together to try to face their innermost problems by interacting with each other. The leader of the group told all of them to face their worst fears. My friend was told to call himself the worst name he could think of, which that particular weekend was "liar." He came out of the weekend session feeling the relief of total exhaustion. And one week later, not a single conflict had been solved.

- *A label is useless.* Any therapeutic dialogue must help someone learn to watch their behavior, their feelings, to understand the various ways of the person in all conditions, with all kinds of people, perhaps making notes on everything that passes through the mind for a whole day or a week. To learn to watch, to see ourselves in action, in relationship, is the point — and to see the need for changing the behavior so new grooves are made in the brain, or new nerve connections, so we can function better.

- *Be aware of weird cult groups that promise instant enlight-enment.* Beware of groups that promise to solve problems by marathon touching or screaming or drugs.

- *Sometimes, with a bit of help you can diagnose your own emotional problems.* Sometimes, this is as difficult as to diagnose the causes of your own physical diseases. If you have a problem that needs attention, do consult someone professionally — your family doctor to begin with, a mental health clinic, a recommended psychiatrist or psychologist or counselor. Treatment may be brief or lengthy. It should provide emotional support, assistance in the development of self-awareness, an understanding of the developmental problems of your particular age, an understanding of moods and their management, and education about the particular symptoms of the illness or problem and their impact on relationships, school, work, and the ability to solve problems and use good judgment.

- *Treatment can be individual or group.* There may possibly be a recommendation for medication. Side effects or possible long-term problems should be explained and understood. Family therapy is an excellent possibility of you happen to have a family that is willing to examine themselves as part of whatever is going on for you. Group therapy helps if your problem is relationships with others; if your problems are relating to yourself, individual therapy might be the best support.

But the word is support, not the creation of a new dependency for you. Be careful of too much authority — look for someone who knows how to lead, not drag your psyche about in chains. You want someone who is empathetic, objective, who can teach you how to change bad habits of behavior for better ones, who uses drugs cautiously but necessarily for the worst of the pain, whose advice you can try but whose power of example is what you learn from. Someone who can show you how to function in the world without being a part of it or separate from it. Someone who can, at last, teach you to teach yourself. Who says, don't hang around leaning on the lamp post, use the light to go on your path ahead.

## Do You Need Help At All?

Obviously, there is a lot of help around, and the trick is to find the right kind. The other trick, of course, is to figure out whether you need help. The only guideline there really is, is whether you are functioning okay. Six extra donuts one day to make you feel better works. Six extra pounds a week is not good. Collecting things instead of attacking every girl you meet is fine. Unless there's no more room in your room to crawl into bed. Being shy at parties can be perfectly normal. Never going to parties at all is a sign of nutsiness. An occasional stress headache is usual. Headaches every time you have to face your math teacher could get you flunked and flipped out. You hate your mother half the time, fine. You hate her all the time, you've got problems. Ditto, your father, brother, or sister. Everybody, including the delivery boy, has to love you, you've got a difficulty. You want no one to get close enough to touch you, you've also got a difficulty.

If over long periods of time your life, with its ups and downs, evens out, you're okay. If you get too lopsided any-where— you get too miserable, you get too full of hate, you get addicted to something, you don't function too well at school or at home— think.

Really think. Therapy or learning how to really have good dialogue (not arguments or exchanges of opinions, just a look at what's going on), can solve problems that only get worse if you wait forever to look at them.

Suppose your parents think emotional disturbances or differences in your brain, sexual orientation, interests, are the equivalent of leprosy. (My child, never! Makes me some kind of failure!) It doesn't matter. Look up Mental Health in the Yellow Pages, and get going. Talk to your school psy-chologist or your family doctor yourself. But try your par-ents first. They may be more sympathetic than you know.

If there is a point to anything in life, it seems to me the most important thing is to understand ourselves so we can understand everybody. We hurt each other a lot.

Psychology, philosophy, the great religious teachers all say the same thing: STOP IT!

Psychology has taught us about the personal experience agenda, the biological/historical agenda, the cultural, social, gender agenda behind human behavior. We can outwit all these agendas by understanding ourselves, the nature of the mind and its conditioning.

Life is complicated.

The human brain is complicated.

We can keep the attitude, however, simple.

We are all constantly laying eggs. They will all produce chickens that will come home to roost. Be careful what you lay — it will come back to give you breakfast or peck you to death in the end.

One more thing. Reading this book will have given you some information. Reading is good learning, but it isn't the same as the flash of psychological insight you get by being aware of your life as you live it every day. Books about psychology may help you understand about psychology, but they don't help you understand about yourselves nearly as well as you yourselves watching yourselves live your life.

You'll discover your peculiarities. You'll discover you really are peculiar. But even you may turn out to be a functional, even awesome human being.

The purpose of psychology is understanding. But the point of understanding is to be connected, to live gloriously. Joy, not pain, is the great teacher.

# Index

# B

# Suggested Reading
# And Selective Bibliography

In this bibliography, only books especially interesting to teenagers are listed. Most of the people and works that are fundamental to contemporary psychology have been mentioned in the text: Sigmund Freud's *Psychopathology of Everyday Life, Interpretation of Dreams,* his notebooks; Carl Jung's *Modern Man in Search of a Soul, Psyche & Symbol;* Erik Erikson's *Childhood and Society* (1963); Peter Blos' *On Adolescence* (1962); Dorothy Briggs' *Your Child's Self-Esteem* (1975); Selma Fraiberg's *The Magic Years* (1959); Arnold Gesell's books, especially *Youth, The Years from Ten to Sixteen* (1956); Theordore Reik, *Listening With the Third Ear* 1975); Karen

Horney, *Self-Analysis* (1968); Margaret Mead, *Coming of Age in Samoa* (1971); Eric Berne, *Games People Play* (1967); Betty Friedan's *The Feminine Mystique* (1964); Elaine Morgan's *The Descent of Women* (1972).

All the works of J. Krishnamurti, especially those on education for the young and young adult such as *Letters to the Schools* (1985). Also *On Right Livelihood* (1992), *The First and Last Freedom* (1954), *Krishnamurti: Reflections on the Self* (1997).

You will want to read psychology textbooks, and studies of mental disorders, books written for parents about teenagers so you understand what they're thinking about you.

A wide variety of writings by scientists in the fields of physics, neurobiology, psychology, sociology, anthropology, religious teachings, philosophy have also informed this book. Major sources for the facts and statistics in this book were newspapers and magazines, government publications, almanacs, public television specials and news broadcasts.

Many books listed have already been mentioned in the text of this book.

*AAUW Report. How Schools Shortchange Girls.* New York: Marlowe & Co., 1995. The American Association of University Women's shocking report about second-class treatment and educational opportunity for girls, grades K-12.

Carlip, Hillary. *Girl Power: Young Women Speak Out!* New York: Warner Books, 1995. Powerful collection of writings by teenage girls, homegirls, schoolgirls, lesbians, jocks, teenage parents, high-risk girls, sorority sisters to gangmembers.

Carlson, Hannah, M.Ed., CRC. *Living with Disabilities, Basic Manuals for Friends of the Disabled*. Madison, CT: Bick Publishing House, 1997. Causes and conditions, psychology of feelings, behaviors, of those in wheelchairs, with mental retardation, mental illness, learning disabilities, more.

Carlson, Dale. *Girls Are Equal Too*. Madison, CT: Bick Publishing House, 1998. A girl can be a fully equal, fully human being if she understands what's behind her, what's facing her, and what to do about it.

Chideya, Farai. *Don't Believe the Hype: Fighting Cultural Misinformation About African Americans*. New York: NAL/Dutton, 1995.

Due, Linnea. *Joining the Tribe: Growing Up Gay & Lesbian*. New York: Doubleday, 1995. Challenges and stigmatism faced by gay, lesbian, bisexual teenagers.

Krishnamurti, J. *The First and Last Freedom*. New York: Harper Collins, 1975. The causes of fear, anger, suffering, loneliness, boredom, the self and its problems — and what to do in relationship to others and to the universe.

Miller, Alice. *Drama of the Gifted Child*. New York: Basic Books, Inc., 1981. The scapegoating and problems of special children.

Riera, Michael. *Surviving High School*. Berkeley, CA: Celestial Arts, 1997. A handbook for navigating the hazards of teenage life: friendships, sex, drugs, driving, family, divorce, suicide.

Rosenberg, Ellen. *Growing Up Feeling Good*. New York: Puffin Books, 1995. Friends, school, sexual decision-making, bodies maturing, family, alcohol and drugs, parents, AIDS, suicide, ethnic diversity, divorce — all the problems faced by teens are covered.

Williams, Greg Alan. *Boys to Men, Maps for the Journey*. New York: Doubleday, 1997. For adolescent and young men to help them deal with the issues that face them.

# Authors

Photo: Monica Feldak

**Dale Carlson**

Author of over fifty books, adult and juvenile, fiction and nonfiction, Carlson has received three ALA Notable Book Awards, and the Christopher Award. She writes novels and psychology books for young adults, and general adult nonfiction. Among her titles are *The Mountain of Truth* (ALA Notable Book), *Where's Your Head?* (Christopher Award), *Girls Are Equal Too* (ALA Notable Book), *Wildlife Care for Birds and Mammals*. Carlson has lived and taught in the Far East: India, Indonesia, China, Japan. She teaches writing and literature during part of each year. She lives in Connecticut with orphaned cats, raccoons, squirrels, and skunks.

Photo: Photos in a Flash

**Hannah Carlson, M.Ed., C.R.C.**

Past Director of Developmental Disabilities at The Kennedy Center for the Mentally Disabled, at West Haven Community House, Hannah Carlson is author of *Living with Disabilities*, based on a six-volume series of Basic Manuals for Friends of the Disabled, including *I Have a Friend with Mental Illness, I Have a Friend with Mental Retardation, I Have a Friend in a Wheelchair, I Have a Friend with Learning Disabilities, I Have a Friend Who Is Blind, I Have a Friend Who Is Deaf.* She is former Senior Therapist and Vocational Counselor/Evaluator at Rusk Institute of Rehabilitation Medicine at New York University Medical Center. She has lectured and taught in her field of the developmentally and traumatically disabled, and is several times published in the international journals "Brain Injury," and in the "Journal of Applied Rehabilitation Counseling." She holds a Masters of Education in Counseling Psychology and a Masters Degree in Developmental Psychology from Columbia University. She is Founder and Director of Discovery Days Day Care Center, and lives with her children Chaney and Shannon and animals of assorted sizes in Connecticut.

# Illustrator

### Carol Nicklaus

Known as a character illustrator, her work has been featured in *The New York Times, Publishers Weekly, Good Housekeeping,* and *Mademoiselle.* To date she has done 150 books for Random House, Golden Press, Atheneum, Dutton, Scholastic, and more. She has won awards from ALA, the Christophers, and The American Institute of Graphic Arts.